For SAMMI

I Hope you find magic in
your life every
day

Tim Faulkner

Magic Molly
The Curse of Cranberry Cottage
By
Trevor Forest

Special thanks to Maureen Vincent-Northam for her marvellous editing skills. Many thanks to Marie Fullerton for designing the wonderful cover and the fabulous illustrations..

I would also like to give a final mention to my Springer Spaniels, Molly and Maisie who have both gone over the Rainbow Bridge. Run Free my darling girls. Run Free.

Doreen. I miss you.

Books by Trevor Forest

Faylinn Frost and the Snow Fairies

Abigail Pink's Angel

Peggy Larkin's War

The Wishnotist

Stanley Stickle Hates Homework

Stanley Stickle Does Not Have A Girlfriend

Stanley Stickle: For One Night Only

Magic Molly: The Mirror Maze

Magic Molly: Gloop

Magic Molly: The Yellow Eye

Magic Molly: Christmas Carole (Christmas Special)

Magic Molly: The Fire Witch

Magic Molly: Halloween Hattie (Halloween Special)

Magic Molly: The Murky Marshes

Magic Molly: The Curse of Cranberry Cottage

http://www.trevorbelshaw.com

Trevor Forest Books on Amazon

For Misty

The best number one fan a writer ever had, thank you for your patience. I kept my promise, here's your book. I hope you like it.

Magic Molly

The Curse of Cranberry Cottage

Chapter One

'Molly Miggins if you aren't downstairs in five minutes flat, your breakfast is going into Harold.'

Molly rolled onto her back and looked at the ceiling. She wasn't sure if Harold, the new in-sink monster she had conjured up a couple of weeks before, liked Wheaty Flakes or not. He seemed to like salad and vegetables best. Anyway, she still thought Harold was a silly name for a former Compost Heap Monster. She had originally called him, Fang, because of his sharp little teeth, but Mrs McCraggity, the housekeeper, had changed it to Harold.

'Fang doesn't like Wheaty Flakes,' she shouted.

'HAROLD, will eat anything if he's hungry enough.' Mrs McCraggity's head appeared around Molly's bedroom door. 'Anyway, Harold's eating habits are irrelevant. Have you forgotten that you're going to stay with Great Aunt Willow this weekend? Granny Whitewand is up and about already; she's really excited about the trip.'

Molly leapt of out bed, and showered and dressed in record time. She slid down the banister to gain an extra few seconds, slipped off the end and bounced on her bottom twice before coming to a halt just in front of the hat stand.

Molly was still rubbing her bottom when she walked into the kitchen. Her packet of Wheaty Flakes was on the table next to a jug of milk and her breakfast bowl.

'Good morning, Millie,' croaked Granny Whitewand who was sitting at the kitchen table holding a cup of tea.

'It's MOLLY, Grandma,' said Molly. Granny Whitewand always got her name wrong. It was an ongoing battle between the two of them.

'So you say,' said Granny Whitewand, as though she knew better.

Molly piled up her bowl with Wheaty Flakes and added a generous sploosh of milk. She picked up her spoon and dug it into the mountain of cereal.

'Are we all staying at Great Aunt Willow's house?' she asked. 'There aren't enough rooms for everyone, are there?'

'She's got plenty of room,' said Granny Whitewand. 'We'll probably have to share, Millie.'

Molly's jaw sagged. Granny Whitewand was an Olympic-class snorer. She decided to have a quiet word with Great Aunt Willow when she got there. The sofa would be a better option than listening to Granny Whitewand's window-rattling snores all night. Especially when her wobbly false teeth clacked together.

'Well, I won't need a room because I'm not going,' said Mrs McCraggity. 'Someone has to stay behind to feed Mr Gladstone and Harold.'

'Jenny will feed Mr Gladstone,' said Molly. Mr Gladstone was Molly's aging and increasingly grumpy cat. Jenny was her best friend.

'It's quite all right,' said the housekeeper. 'I don't mind staying. Harold has to be fed throughout the day. You can't just feed an in-sink monster morning and night; he has to have regular meals.'

Molly grinned. Mrs McCraggity had really fallen under her in-sink monster's spell. As if to prove the point she held half a slice of hot-buttered toast over the hole of what used to be the in-sink food disposal unit. A green head with saucer-like eyes popped out of the open hole.

'Good morning, Harold,' said Mrs McCraggity. 'I've saved you a bit of my toast. There'll be more later when Mr and Mrs Miggins have had breakfast. There might even be a rind or two of bacon if you're lucky.'

Harold climbed out of the dark sink hole. He was a good looking monster, as monsters go. He had little pointy ears, long green fingers and toes and a fat little tummy. He grabbed the toast and took a huge bite.

'Yum, Fang likes toast,' said Harold.

'Erm, I think you'll find your name is Harold,' said the housekeeper.

'Harold likes toast,' said Fang. He stuffed the rest of it into his mouth, chewed at it with his needle sharp teeth.

'Burrrrrrp. 'scuse me, missus.'

Mrs McCraggity stroked him behind the ears. Harold closed his eyes and made a contented noise.

'You spoil that creature, Mrs M,' said Granny Whitewand.

The housekeeper stopped stroking Harold and folded her arms across her bosom. 'I do not spoil him. I'm just making sure he gets enough to eat. Had someone other than Molly used that Compost Heap Monster spell, he could be sitting under a mound of rotting cabbage in someone's garden. It breaks my heart to think about it.'

Granny Whitewand's knees sounded as though someone had just fired off two pistols as she got to her feet. Molly winced. The old witch crossed to the sink and offered the half-drunk cup of her tea to the in-sink monster.

'Here you go, Fang. Strong and sweet, just how you like it.'

Fang took the tea cup and drained it in one long gulp. 'That's hit the spot, missus,' he said with a grin.

Granny Whitewand cackled, then sucked her wobbly teeth back into place. 'He's picking up my little sayings nicely.'

'You'll confuse the poor little mite if you keep calling him Fang,' said the housekeeper. 'His name is Harold.' She waited until Harold had finished licking the cup, then she took it gently from the monster's hands. 'Careful, Harold, we don't want to drop Mrs Miggins' best china do we?'

'No missus,' said Harold.

'I think I'll get you a plastic beaker to drink tea out of,' said Mrs McCraggity thoughtfully. She carefully dunked the china cup into the washing up suds in the big sink and washed it gently with her rubber-glove covered hands.

Molly chased the last few Wheaty Flakes around her bowl and dropped the spoon into it with a clatter. 'I'm off to see Dad,' she said. 'He owes me some extra pocket money for helping clean the car yesterday.'

'Hang on, Millie,' said Granny Whitewand. 'I could do with a hand with my luggage.'

'I'll come to your room after I've seen Dad… and my name is MOLLY, Grandma.'

'Your mother should have called you Gertie, then we wouldn't have any confusion,' said Granny Whitewand.

'I'm glad she didn't,' said Molly. She pulled a face. 'Anyway, there isn't any confusion. My name is Molly.'

'That's not what it says on our coven register,' said the old witch.

'THAT'S BECAUSE YOU WROTE THE NAMES IN THE REGISTER,' shouted Molly. She left the kitchen before her grandmother could come up with a reply and skipped down the corridor towards her father's study.

Mr Miggins, or the Great Rudolpho as he was also known, was a stage magician who used real magic in his tricks. Molly's mother was the High Witch at the White Academy that Molly attended.

Their studies were at either end of a short passage. To the right of Mr Miggins' door was a tall perch on which sat a colourful parrot. The parrot was actually dead but he had refused to cross over to the other side and spent his time guarding the corridor. He claimed to be the world's foremost, security parrot. On the windowsill at its side, was a photograph album.

'Halt, who goes there?' The parrot held up one wing and made a slow down motion with it.

'You know who it is, parrot,' said Molly, who had had many a run in with the bird.

'If I knew, I wouldn't be asking, would I?' he replied.

Molly sighed. She was used to the ritual but it didn't get any less annoying.

'I'm Molly Miggins and I've come to see my dad, who is in his room waiting to give me some money.'

The parrot turned its attention to the photo album. On the cover, in big letters, were the words "MOST WANTED". He opened it with a wing tip and began to flick through the pages. Most of the photographs were pictures he had cut out of a catalogue, but one was a full-page, blow up of Molly in her witch's uniform.

'Money eh?' He tapped the photograph and narrowed his eyes. 'So you admit you are about to attempt to BLACKMAIL professor Miggins.'

'Don't be stupid all of your life,' said Molly. 'Have one day off at least.'

The parrot tapped the picture with his wing tip. 'I happen to have had a tipoff that a world renowned, criminal is in the area, and the description fits...' The parrot looked around the room, then scowled and pointed a wing tip at Molly. 'YOU!'

Molly folded her arms across her chest and tapped her foot. 'You're being ridiculous now; I've had enough of this.'

'Oh, go on,' said the parrot. 'Play the game a bit.'

Molly suddenly felt sorry for the parrot. He did spend most of his time alone.

'Oh, go on then,' she said. 'Who am I supposed to be?'

'Desperate Doris, the despicable doyenne of deception,' said the parrot.

Molly sighed. 'All right then.'

The parrot held up the book and showed the picture to Molly.

'So, Desperate Doris, we meet again,' he croaked, menacingly.

Molly played along. 'How did you track me down so quickly?'

'There was one little thing that gave you away,' said the parrot.

'What was that?' asked Molly.

'Your brain,' said the parrot. 'Mine is so much bigger than yours so it was easy to follow the clues.'

'Okay, parrot, you win,' said Molly. She made a move towards the door of her father's study.

'I can't let you go in there,' said the parrot.

'Why not?' asked Molly.

'Because you're Desperate Doris, the despicable doyenne of deception,' said the parrot.

'No I'm not,' said Molly.

'YOU JUST ADMITTED IT,' yelled the parrot.

'THAT WAS A GAME,' shouted Molly.

'I RECORDED OUR CONVERSATION, I HAVE THE EVIDENCE,' screamed the parrot.

'YOU'RE MAD,' yelled Molly.

Just then the study door opened and out walked a bewildered Professor Miggins. 'What on earth is going on out here?' he asked.

The parrot inspected its foot and whistled. Molly glared at the bird.

'I've come to get the extra pocket money you owe me, Dad. I want to put it with the holiday money I've saved.'

'Money?' Mr Miggins looked confused. The parrot eyed Molly suspiciously.

'For helping, yesterday,' said Molly.

'Oh, yes I remember,' said the professor. He pulled out his wallet and handed Molly a five-pound note. 'There you go, Molly. I'll see you out the front in half an hour or so. I just want to finish my notes.' Mr Miggins walked back into his study and closed the door behind him.

Molly walked towards the corridor but just before she reached the corner she turned to face the parrot. She waved the five pound note in the air and stuck out her tongue, then she turned away with the parrot's angry voice screeching in her ears.

'Blackmailer,' he squawked. 'I'll get you next time, Desperate Doris.'

Chapter Two

When Molly stuck her head around Granny Whitewand's door to let her know there was going to be thirty-minute delay, her ears were assailed by the highest pitched whistling snore she had ever heard in her life. Granny Whitewand was a champion snorer but this effort was window shatteringly loud. Molly backed away, closed the door, then wiggled her fingers in her ears and shook her head to clear it. She walked back along the passageway and stopped at the kitchen door. Mrs McCraggity was leant over the kitchen sink whispering to Harold.

'There you are, Harold, a big fat juicy sausage, just for you. Don't let on I cooked it for you, you're only meant to have leftovers.'

Harold stuck the whole sausage into his mouth and smiled with delight.

'I'm just going up to the newsagents, Mrs M,' said Molly.

Mrs McCraggity almost leapt out of her skin. She turned around holding her hand against her chest.

'Oh, Molly, you did give me a start. I was just giving Harold a little treat… he needs some protein… I'm not spoiling him…'

'Your secret is safe with me.' Molly grinned at the housekeeper. 'If anyone wants me I'm getting sweets and magazines for the journey. I'll be back in ten minutes.'

Molly found there were two magazines waiting to be picked up from behind the counter at the newsagents. Mr Tidings, the newsagent, handed them over to Molly with a smile.

'There you are, Miss Miggins. One copy of "My Broom" and one copy of "Cauldron". Plenty to read on your journey.'

Molly paid for her magazines and bought a bag of chewy sweets for the journey. They weren't really her favourites but Granny Whitewand was a sweet monster and usually ate more than Molly did. She couldn't steal chewy ones though; they stuck her wobbly teeth together.

As Molly stepped out of the shop she heard the screech of car brakes followed by a voice that sent a shudder down her spine.

'Molly Miggins! Wait there, I want to talk to you.'

Molly looked across the pavement to the pure white Rolls Royce car that had pulled up in the middle of the road. A door opened and Henrietta Havelots, the richest girl in the county, leapt out of the car and, ignoring the beeping traffic behind her, walked slowly across to Molly. When she reached the pavement the chauffeur drove on and pulled up a few yards further along.

'Hello, Poor Girl,' said Henrietta cheerfully. She eyed Molly's magazines. 'What have we here then?'

'Just my monthly magazines,' replied Molly. 'Nothing you'd be interested in.'

'You're probably right. I have a subscription to Posh Pony magazine. My new pony, Princess Primula was featured in it last month. They sent a man to take pictures and interview me. It was jolly interesting, you should order it... mind you, it is rather expensive for the likes of you. It would be six months' worth of your pocket money, I imagine.'

Henrietta sighed. 'It must be incredibly frustrating being poor. We go to the Maldives for our holidays, we have a villa there. Sometimes we go to the Cote D'azur. If we get bored, we call for the yacht and go sailing around the Greek islands. Only the nice ones though, not those touristy places.' Henrietta screwed up her nose at the thought. 'I bet you go to those touristy places don't you? Or can't you afford a holiday?'

'I'm going on holiday today actually,' said Molly.

Henrietta looked Molly up and down. 'You don't look like you're going on holiday, I mean, you haven't had your hair done, you're wearing the same clothes you always wear. You look like you've just nipped out to the shop.'

'I have just nipped out to the shop,' replied Molly. 'We're just having a few days away and I don't need a haircut anyway, I like my hair as it is.'

'Really! A *few* days?' Henrietta's eyes opened wide. 'We don't go anywhere for a *few* days, it's hardly worth the effort. You probably can't afford a fortnight away though.' She pulled a sad face. 'So, where is this fabulous place? I bet I've been there already. I've been everywhere, at least twice.'

'We're going to stay with Great Aunt Willow in Woodhenge, as it happens,' said Molly. 'It will be really interesting, there's lots to do. I love going there.'

Henrietta's brow creased into a dozen lines. 'Woodhenge?'

'You won't have heard of it,' said Molly. 'It's very exclusive. They don't let just anyone stay there.' She pushed her magazines under her arm and turned away.

Henrietta grabbed hold of Molly's cloak and held it fast. 'Where abouts is this place? I bet I have been there, if it's exclusive I must have been. We stay in all the best places.'

'It's a little village on the coast,' said Molly. She tried to walk away but Henrietta held her back.

'Which coast? The French coast, Spanish coast, Italian, African?'

'English, south coast,' said Molly. 'It's a lovely place, full of thatched cottages, it has a nice little village green and it's only a few hundred yards from a quiet, sandy bay. It's nice and peaceful, not touristy at all.'

'Boriiiiiiiiiiiiiiiiiiing,' Henrietta let go of Molly's cloak. 'It could at least have a theme park or something.'

'That would spoil it,' said Molly. 'It's perfect as it is. There's an ancient, magic circle, a bit like Stonehenge but made out of wood… actually the wood's all rotted away now, but you can still see where–'

'Boriiiiiiiiiiiiing.'

'It's not boring at all, it's a very magical place,' replied Molly. 'There are only a hundred or so houses and most of the families have lived there for centuries.'

'Boriiiiiiiiiiiiing'

Molly turned away and began walking down the hill. After a few yards she looked back over her shoulder. 'I'll have a good time anyway. I'm going to have a close up look at Cranberry Cottage. People say it's one of the scariest places in England.'

'Scary? What's so scary about it?' Henrietta stared after Molly.

Molly stopped and turned around to face her. 'That's what I intend to find out. Granny Whitewand and Great Aunt Willow have never let me go near the place before, but I'm going to see it close up this time. All I know is, it was once lived in by an evil witch called Belladonna Blackheart.'

'Woodhenge hey?' Henrietta was suddenly very thoughtful. 'Cranberry Cottage does sound rather intriguing.'

'It does, doesn't it,' replied Molly with an air of superiority. 'The cottage has a curse on it apparently. I'm going to have so much fun exploring; you can keep your Mouldy Dives.'

'Maldives,' Henrietta corrected her, but Molly wasn't listening. She walked down the hill with a huge grin on her face.

Chapter Three

When Molly got home she found that a new, updated spell book had been delivered by the White Witch's Academy postman. Molly had a quick flick through it while drinking juice at the kitchen table. She pulled Wonky, her twisted, ancient wand from the secret pocket of her cloak and addressed him silently. His fat, friendly little face appeared about three quarters of the way along its length.

Wonky was actually a world famous wand called Cedron, and he had cast the final spell that sent the Black Witch, Morgana, and the entire Black Academy of witches to a place called The Void, during Witch-Wars, hundreds of years before. Molly was very proud to own such a famous wand and the pair had bonded into something that went far beyond friendship. It was hoped that the Black Witches would be sealed in forever, but Molly had, on several occasions, been forced to thwart Morgana's attempts to escape the dark emptiness of The Void and return to the real world.

'Good morning, Molly Miggins,' said the wand. 'Do we have a new book of spells to peruse?'

'We do, Wonky,' said Molly. 'I've just had a quick look through, there doesn't appear to be anything wildly exciting this time.' She pointed one or two out.

'All of them have their uses, Molly Miggins,' replied the wand. 'There are some very powerful ones in this volume. Hurricane, for instance, will whip up a really fierce local storm and Polar Storm will bring snow on the warmest of days. Energise will rapidly replace your energy levels and Zoom will move you quickly over a short distance.'

'What's this one here, Wonky?' Molly pointed to a spell that had no description underneath.

'Replay?' Wonky's face took on a quizzical look. 'Hmm, I think that could be a brand new spell. It's not in my built in database at least. Perhaps it's a spell the Wizard from the Magic Council has made up and he's put it in the new volume for field testing.'

Molly nodded. It seemed like the kind of thing the Wizard would do. He was always giving Molly difficult tasks to perform, some of them extremely dangerous. Although she complained about it she knew he had her best interests at heart, and she had been rapidly promoted through the witch grades as a result of successfully completing the tasks.

Molly pointed to a spell called, Instant Weariness, make your opponent feel extremely tired. 'That looks like fun, Wonky; I could use that on Henrietta when she starts on one of her long boasty speeches.'

'Come on, Molly, it's time to go.' Molly's mum called from the hall.

Molly slipped Wonky into the secret pocket of her cloak, rushed out into the hallway and stuffed the spell book and magazines into her back pack, then she picked up her small suitcase and carried it out to the car. Granny Whitewand was already in her seat.

'Hurry up, Millie,' she croaked excitedly. 'You're holding us all up.'

'Millie isn't, MOLLY is holding us all up,' replied Molly, a little testily. Dad's not here yet, anyway and he's driving today.'

Granny Whitewand fidgeted about on the back seat. 'Well, hurry up anyway, it will be night time before we get there at this rate.' She pointed back into the house. My case is in my room. It's a bit heavy for me.'

Molly sighed and walked back into the house. Granny Whitewand's door was open and Mr Miggins was inside struggling with an enormous trunk.

'She must have packed everything, including the kitchen sink in here.' He puffed out his cheeks. 'Give me a hand with it, Molly.'

With the Professor dragging at one end and Molly pushing at the other, the pair managed to manoeuvre the huge trunk out to the car. They had to get help from Mr Blower, one of their neighbours, to get it into the back of the people carrier.

'Blimey!' he panted, when the trunk had finally been lifted into the back. 'What have you got in there? Rocks?'

'Just a few essentials.' Granny Whitewand tossed her head and looked out of the window. 'You never know when you're going to need something. So I make sure I take everything, then I've always got everything I need.'

Molly blew out her cheeks and climbed into the car. The rear seats were set out opposite each other. Molly put her backpack on the centre seat and sat on the one next to the window, facing Granny Whitewand. Mr and Mrs Miggins climbed into the front and with a toot of thanks to Mr Blower, they pulled out of the drive and onto the street.

By the time they had got to the end of the road, Granny Whitewand was snoring. The levels were not up to her window-rattling best, but it was bad enough for Molly to screw up couple of tissues from the box on the console and stuff them in her ears. They hung almost to her neck, like a pair of long, paper earrings.

Not long after, they left the town and headed out to the motorway. Molly soon got bored watching the traffic pass by and opened one of her magazines. She checked Granny Whitewand wasn't just pretending to be asleep and stuffed a chewy, caramel into her mouth. As if she suspected she was missing something, Granny Whitewand suddenly jerked her head forward, her eyes flashed open.

'Are we nearly there yet?' she croaked.

'We've not long set off,' called Mrs Miggins from the front seat.

Granny Whitewand stared out of the window as if she knew better. A big blue sign informed them that the turn off for Leicester was a mere ten miles away.

'Is Leicester near Woodhenge?' she asked Molly.

Molly tried to hide the fact that she was eating a toffee and shook her head.

'How far is it then?'

'Dunnoffff,' Molly mumbled, melted caramel running down her chin.

Granny Whitewand's eyes narrowed. 'Are you surreptitiously munching sweets?' she demanded to know.

Molly shook her head and concentrated on the traffic.

Granny Whitewand leaned forward in her seat and studied Molly intently. 'What's that running down your chin then?'

Molly took a huge breath and swallowed the toffee in one gulp. She opened her mouth wide, pointed to it with the index finger of her right hand while the left hand pushed the bag of toffees behind her back. The sweets wouldn't last five minutes, let alone the whole trip if Granny Whitewand found out about them. She had been known to take out her false teeth and masticate the toffee between her rock hard gums. The smacking, slurping noise she made was utterly horrible.

The old witch seemed satisfied and leaned back into her seat. Two minutes later she was snoring again, her head facing the roof of the car, her neck perched on the back of the seat.

Molly watched, fascinated as her grandmother took in a deep, wheezy breath, there was a few moments of total silence before the air escaped from her mouth in a high-pitched, whistle, followed by a series of deep grunts that would have outdone the prize winning pig in a truffle snuffling contest.

Molly suddenly had an idea. She pulled another tissue from the box and tore off a five-centimetre strip, she waited until the grunts had finished and the wheezing air intake had begun, before reaching forward and dropping the strip of paper onto her grandmother's lips.

As the air escaped, the paper feather floated up into the air until it hovered a good foot above the old witch's mouth. When the whistle subsided, the strip of paper floated slowly down until it almost touched her lips, then the whole process started again. Molly giggled, pushed another toffee into her mouth, and watched the rise and fall of the ribbon of paper. After five minutes, she got bored and went back to reading her magazine. She had just popped two more toffees into her mouth when she heard a choking sound and Granny Whitewand shot forward in her seat. She pulled the piece of tissue from her mouth, stared at it with a confused look on her face, then screwed it up and stuffed it into her pocket.

'Are we nearly there yet?' she asked.

'Not yet, Granny Whitewand,' called Mr Miggins from the front.

The old witch looked out of the window and read the big blue road sign. Northampton 20 miles.

'Is Northampton near Woodhenge, Millie?' she asked.

'Nommmffff.' Molly shook her head.

Granny Whitewand looked at her, suspiciously.

'Are you sure you're not eating a sweetie?' she asked.

Molly's cheeks bloated out as she pushed the toffees to the sides of her mouth.

'Let's play a game of I Spy,' said Granny Whitewand. She looked around the car then back to Molly. 'I spy with my crafty, beady, see-everything, little eye, something beginning with... F.'

Molly turned her head away and gulped down the caramels.

'Floor,' she said.

'No.'

Molly's eyes rested on the large metal flask that had Granny Whitewand's hot, sweet tea supply inside.

'Flask,' she said.

'No.'

'I don't know then.' Molly gave up.

'F is for FIBBER!' Granny Whitewand launched herself forward and pulled Molly's arm from behind her back, spilling the bag of toffees onto the carpet.

'You don't like them,' yelled Molly desperately. 'They stick your teeth together.'

'I'll just try one,' cackled Granny Whitewand... 'then I'll try another, and another...'

Molly was saved when Mrs Miggins passed a tube of extra strong mints over the headrest.

'I got these for you, Granny Whitewand, you like mints.'

Molly breathed a huge sigh of relief and passed the roll of sweets to her grandmother who tore open the packet, pushed three large mints into her mouth and sucked on them noisily. Molly picked up her own sweets, pulled bits of carpet fluff from them and dropped them back into the paper bag.

Three long hours later, that included two toilet stops, one travel-sick stop and twenty-seven queries as to whether they were 'nearly there yet', Mr Miggins pulled the car off the motorway and headed along a road that was little more than a country track. Granny Whitewand seemed to sense the decreased speed and sat up in her seat again.

'Are we nearly–?'

'YES!' screamed Molly, 'we *ARE* nearly there. Look!' she pointed to a rickety wooden signpost at the side of the road that read: Woodhenge, 5 miles.

Granny Whitewand began to fidget in her seat.

'Ooh, I can't wait to see Willow; I've missed her so much. It's been ages since we got together.'

'It was two weeks ago,' said Molly. 'She came over for cousin Lavinia's wedding. You argued with her the whole time she was here.'

'No I didn't.' Granny Whitewand sniffed. 'We get on really well, me and Willow, everyone knows that.'

'You're at each other's throats as soon as you clap eyes on each other,' replied Molly. 'You argue about everything.'

'We're very close,' said the old witch. 'We always were, even as kids.'

'Didn't you once set her bloomers alight with a *HotBot* spell?' asked Molly.

Granny Whitewand cackled. 'Oh yes, that was so good. She had to run to the village pond and sit in it. You could see the steam rising.' She cackled again. 'Those were the days,' she said.

The car slowed to a stop and Mr Miggins opened the driver's side door then leaned back inside.

'We're here,' he called.

Granny Whitewand waited impatiently for Mr Miggins to release the child lock on her door, she moved surprisingly quickly for an ancient old crone and was outside on the grass verge before Molly had stuffed her magazine and two remaining toffees into her backpack.

Aunt Willow's house was a two-storey affair with large windows, a slate roof and ivy covering the entire front wall. Mrs Miggins opened a small wooden gate and led the way along a flower-bordered, crazy-paved path to the red-painted front door which opened before Molly's mum could use the large, brass knocker.

'Hello, hello, hello,' gushed the white haired old witch that stood in the doorway. Her dark grey hat was leaning back at a ridiculous angle, her hair hung in straggles around a thin, long-nosed face. Her mouth was smeared with lipstick and six, long hairs hung from a squidgy-looking, green wart on her chin.

'It's so lovely to see you all, it's been far too long,' she gushed.

'It's been two weeks,' muttered Molly.

Granny Whitewand launched herself through the crowd and hugged her sister. 'Willow, oh, Willow, you can't know, how much I've missed you.'

Granny Whitewand pulled away, both sisters had tears flowing down their cheeks. Molly sighed and waited for the inevitable.

'You've messed up your lipstick,' said Granny Whitewand.

'At least I'm wearing some, I made the effort, unlike some I could mention,' Aunt Willow replied.

'Well, are you going to invite us in, or leave us standing on the doorstep all night?' asked Granny Whitewand.

'I'll let the others in, I might leave you there,' said Great Aunt Willow. 'You make too much mess, it takes me ages to clean up after you, even if I use a deep clean spell.'

'Oh, the cheek of it,' Granny Whitewand's voice was raised a notch. 'Your house is so dirty I have to wipe my feet on the way OUT!'

Before Great Aunt Willow could respond, Molly pushed her way between them and plonked her bag down on the dining room table. 'What's for lunch? I'm starving, and I want to know why you never let me go anywhere near Cranberry Cottage,' she said.

Chapter Four

'Pass the cake-plate please, Molly.' Great Aunt Willow held out a thin, wrinkly hand.

Molly picked up the large, white plate and passed it to her mother, who passed it to Mr Miggins, who passed it to their host who sat at the end of the table, directly opposite and as far away as they could arrange, from Granny Whitewand, who sat at the other end.

Great Aunt Willow cut herself a dainty sized piece of seed cake and put it onto a small plate on the table in front of her. She took a fork, broke off the tiniest of chunks and manoeuvred it carefully towards her mouth, her other hand held underneath to catch any crumbs. At the other end of the table, Granny Whitewand pushed a huge slab of Madeira cake into her mouth, and when she spoke, crumbs sprayed everywhere.

'Cranberry Cottage is a dangerous place and you shouldn't go anywhere near it, Millie.'

'Who's Millie?' asked Great Aunt Willow, looking around in case someone else had entered the room.

'She means me,' Molly held up her hand. Aunt Willow knew exactly who Granny Whitewand meant.

'Well, she might have got your name wrong, but she's right about Cranberry Cottage. Stay away from there, Molly. It's not a nice place… It's cursed.'

'I know that,' said Molly. 'But I don't know why it's cursed. I want to know the whole story. I'm old enough now and I'm a qualified witch.'

'You're still a junior, Millie,' said Granny Whitewand. 'You're not powerful enough to go into that place, even if you could get in, which you can't. None of us is powerful enough. Just stay away, it's for the best.'

'But, aren't you intrigued by it?' Molly looked from Great Aunt Willow to her grandmother, and back.

'Oh we're intrigued all right,' said Granny Whitewand, 'we're just not silly enough to bother the ghost of Belladonna Blackheart, that's all.'

'I want to know all about it,' said Molly. 'I'll only log onto the Witcher website on the Internet if you don't tell me.'

'You and that pesky Intynut thingy,' replied Granny Whitewand. 'You're obsessed with it.'

'It's only the same as reading The Witcher in book form. The only difference is, I read it on a computer,' said Molly.

Great Aunt Willow sighed and got to her feet. 'Come on then, I'll make a fresh pot of tea and we'll sit in the lounge and tell you all about Cranberry Cottage, but you have to promise us that you won't try to go in there yourself, Molly. Some things are best left alone.'

The lounge was small, with a two-seater sofa, two wing-backed chairs and a round coffee table set between them. Molly sat on a cushion on the floor by the door while Mrs Miggins poured the tea from a white, flower-patterned china pot. She poured milk into a cup, added one lump of sugar and passed it to Willow. Aunt Willow took a sip, smiled in thanks and held the dainty cup between both hands on her lap.

'How much do you know about the Witch Wars, Molly?' she asked.

'I know everything about it. I did a project at the Academy. I got an A+ for it.' Molly looked pleased with herself.

'I doubt you know everything about it, there's a lot more to know than you think.' Aunt Willow took another sip of tea and put her cup and saucer on the coffee table. Mrs Miggins handed Granny Whitewand a large mug, only half full in case she spilled it.

'Five sugar lumps?' the old witch asked.

Mrs Miggins nodded, 'Just how you like it.'

When they were all settled, Great Aunt Willow continued.

'As I was saying, you might know the general history of the Witch Wars but you don't know it all. No one does. There are bits and pieces of evidence lying around, bits and pieces of handed down, first hand statements, but nothing written down officially, unless the Wizard at the Magic Council has anything... Anyway, basically everyone thinks that the entire Black Academy was banished to the deepest depths of The Void, but that isn't true. At least one of the witches escaped before The Void was sealed. Belladonna Blackheart certainly did.'

'Hang on,' said Molly. 'I think Wonky might like to hear this, he was there at the time, after all.'

Molly pulled her wand from her secret pocket and addressed it. Wonky's fat little face appeared three quarters of the way along the shaft.

'Hello Molly Miggins, is it story time?' he asked.

'It is, Wonky,' replied Molly. 'We're just hearing about Belladonna Blackheart.'

'She was a nasty piece of work,' said Wonky. 'She was Morgana's right hand witch.'

'Did you know she escaped The Void, Wonky?'

'I had a feeling that someone had,' the wand replied. 'But casting that final spell exhausted me, burned me, damaged me so much that I had to rest up for a long, long time to recover.'

Molly smiled fondly at her wand. 'And you were put in a case, on a shelf at the Academy and were forgotten about for hundreds of years, until the day we met.'

Wonky smiled. 'And the rest is history.' He looked across the room at Aunt Willow. 'So, it was Belladonna who escaped? That is bad news. Where did she go?'

'Here, of all places.' Aunt Willow waved her hand towards the window. 'Cranberry Cottage to be exact.'

'Why here though?' asked Molly.

'Because it was out of the way and no one would know who she was, what she'd done in the past and what she would get up to in the future,' said Willow. 'Where better really? There were only about thirty families living here back then. She disguised herself well enough to fool them all. She had the cottage built and lived among the villagers as though she'd always been here. But, she held a dark secret. She was charged with the task of opening The Void and sending signals into it to help guide Morgana and the rest of the Black Witches. No one knows how far she got with it. She couldn't have been successful, because, as we all know, Morgana is still in The Void. Mainly thanks to our Molly.'

Aunt Willow smiled fondly at her Great Niece.

Molly smiled back. 'So, what's all the fuss about, she's long dead isn't she? Why is the cottage so dangerous?'

'That's just the thing, Millie,' Granny Whitewand took a deep slurp of tea, smacked her lips and leaned back on the sofa. 'We don't think she is dead, not properly dead at least. We think she's still in there, waiting for something to happen, something that will allow her to carry on with her business.'

'Not properly dead... Oh, you mean like the parrot at home?' Molly nodded her head as if she understood.

'Not quite, Millie.' Granny Whitewand looked from Willow to Mrs Miggins, then back to Molly. 'We believe she's a wraith, it's a sort of living ghost, something not properly dead and not properly alive, something that might be able to come back if it is given the energy. We think that she was very close to opening The Void when she lost her strength. We think she's still there, just waiting to seize any opportunity available to her.'

'So, why hasn't the Wizard at the Magic Council been informed? He could do something surely?'

'He can't, Millie, he did try, many years ago now, but even he couldn't get in. No one can get in. There's a spell on the place, a spell so powerful or so crafty that no member of our coven, Willow's coven, or even the Magic Council, have ever been able to work it out. On top of that she cursed it in her last moments. She cast a spell that said anyone who entered would be thrown into The Void to spend the rest of their days hiding from Morgana and her Black Army. You'd have to know the exact words she used before the curse could be lifted and she won't tell anyone what they were, even if they could find her.'

Molly sat quietly for a moment. 'So, the locals didn't know anything about all this, only witches know?'

Granny Whitewand slurped the last of her tea and wiped her mouth on the sleeve of her cloak. 'Again, not quite. The locals knew all about what happened. As she grew older, I mean, seriously older – she was already very old when she came to live here – she got a little bit forgetful and more than a bit odd. She forgot herself and would fly her broom on the full moon. She cast hexes on the local population and soured the milk, ruined their crops. In the end they got fed up of her and came with flaming torches to burn the cottage to the ground.'

'So, how come it's still there?' asked Molly.

'They couldn't set it alight,' said Aunt Willow. 'They couldn't damage a single bit of thatch. She'd cast a spell so powerful that nothing could damage the place. The Parish Council has tried to demolish it five times over the years, but they always have to give up. The last attempt was fifty years ago. They bought in bulldozers and explosives. The blasts broke widows for miles around but Cranberry Cottage remained untouched. In the end, the council built a big, iron-railed fence around the grounds and tried to forget about it. That's why you won't find any mention of it in the tourist guides. It's a secret they want kept between as few people as possible.'

'Why though? Surely they can make a lot of money from the tourists,' said Molly, 'and why is it dangerous? If she's sealed in and no one else can get inside, what's the problem?'

'She's not sealed in, Molly,' said Mrs Miggins. 'We believe she can move about in her own grounds but not anywhere beyond. She's been spotted moving about in the garden over the years, especially on a full moon. Her spell doesn't work outside of the cottage boundary. This is the reason we want you to keep away. We believe Belladonna is just waiting for someone to stray into her lair. She has the power to take the energy from a young, strong victim and use it herself. If she does manage to trap someone she'll be back in all her dark, glory and who knows what mischief she'll get up to.'

Molly blew out her cheeks.

'So, now you understand why we can't allow you to go anywhere near that place, Molly,' said Aunt Willow. If Belladonna got hold of a witch, especially a clever, powerful young witch like you, there would be no stopping her. She'd bring Morgana back from The Void, and we'd probably never see you again.'

Chapter Five

Later in the afternoon, Molly and her mum and dad took a walk down the cliff path to find a beautiful, almost deserted, sandy beach that ran the full length of a horse-shoe, shaped bay. Mr and Mrs Miggins rolled out their beach towels and sat down to enjoy the warmth of the late afternoon sun while Molly explored the many rock pools that littered the shoreline. On the way back, they took a path that led up a winding track to the cliff top. They walked through a small wood until they came to a wide, green meadow; the field was overgrown and the grass came up to Molly's knees. There was an area in the middle of the meadow where the grass was patchier and grew in clumps. In the centre was a circle made up of dark, oddly shaped marks.

'These marks are where huge wooden posts used to sit, Molly,' explained Mrs Miggins. 'It looked a lot like Stonehenge but instead of building it out of huge pieces of stone, they used wood. It has all rotted away now, sadly. The ancient people who built it used to conduct magical ceremonies here, especially at midsummer and midwinter.'

Molly strolled around the perimeter of the circle. 'It must have looked awesome as you approached it,' she said. Molly walked to the very centre of the circle and pulled her wand from the secret pocket of her cloak. She addressed it silently and Wonky's fat little face appeared.

'Hello, Molly Miggins, are we having a history lesson?'

'Sort of, Wonky,' replied Molly. 'The magic in this place is even older than you.'

'Indeed it is,' said Wonky, 'can you feel it?'

'Not really,' said Molly. 'I think the spells are long gone.'

'Close your eyes and concentrate,' said the wand.

Molly closed her eyes and held Wonky high above her head. For a full minute nothing happened, but then a thick mist appeared out of nowhere, and from it came the muffled sound of chanting. Molly held her breath as a line of people dressed in long white robes, stepped out of the haze. The leader of the group sported a long, white beard and held a sturdy-looking ash staff, he reminded Molly of the Wizard from the Magic Council. The people behind carried platters of food and pots of water. When the mist had completely cleared, Molly could see the full majesty of the huge, thick, wooden pillars. The line of druids marched around them until they came to the tallest pair of the timber posts. They turned inwards and walked slowly to the centre where Molly stood, next to a broad, plinth that looked like a long table. The lead druid stepped aside and the followers laid out their gifts on the podium. The druid with the ash shaft pointed it to the skies and spoke in a strange language. The crowd knelt, then bowed down until their foreheads touched the floor. The leader called out another incantation and struck the plinth three times with the ash rod. Gradually, the skies began to darken, Molly knew what was happening straight away, she'd seen a solar eclipse when she was on holiday in Wales.

When the eclipse was at its darkest, the lead druid knelt in front of the plinth and chanted a string of strange words. As a beam of light shone through the tallest pair of wooden pillars he got to his feet and raised the rod above his head with both hands. He turned away from the still-bowing people and looked straight at Molly. He lowered his eyes to the floor and dropped his chin to his chest.

'I see you, lady of the light,' he said.

Molly was shocked, she had no idea how to respond so she just said, 'I see you too, druid.'

The druid pointed his ash rod towards the ever brightening sky and spoke again to Molly.

'Lady of the light, we thank you for returning the sun to us. We see your power. We bring offerings to thank you for slaying the demon that took away the light.'

'I didn't do anyth–'

'We thank you for our beasts, we thank you for our crops, we thank you for the gift of children. We beg you, keep us safe from the spirits of the darkness.'

Molly opened her mouth to speak again, but Wonky shook his head. 'Molly Miggins, to them you are the spirit of the light. They believe it whatever reply you give. It's probably best just to smile, or nod.'

Molly looked at the druid, smiled and nodded. 'Thank you,' she said.

The druid raised the rod again and turned around three times chanting an ancient spell. A gentle breeze began to blow on the outskirts of the circle. The breeze picked up speed until the grass at the edge of the circle became flattened, then it picked up intensity again until it blew at almost storm force around the standing timbers. At the centre Molly stood with her mouth open. There wasn't as much as a gentle zephyr inside the circle. When the swirling wind was at its ferocious height, the druid turned back to Molly.

'Our circle protects us from the demons of darkness. Goodness and light is captured here; no evil will endure while the spirit of light watches over us. Gwitha war kelgh.'

Gradually, the vision began to fade. Molly opened her eyes to find that she was still in the centre of the circle. Mr and Mrs Miggins walked around the perimeter, chatting to each other about the age of the site and had obviously not been part of the magical vision. Molly lowered her arm and stared at her wand.

'WOW! That was amazing, Wonky. What was that all about? It was very strange.'

'Old magic never dies, Molly Miggins,' replied the wand. 'It just becomes harder to see. The words the Druid chanted means, "watch over the circle". It's a sort of protection spell. The people feel safe inside this place. They believed nothing with evil intent could have any power over them while they were inside it.'

'I've never been given offerings before,' said Molly. 'It was a very humbling experience. I just wanted to tell them there was no need for them to do it.'

'But they felt there was a need, Molly Miggins. They believed that they had to do it to keep their magic alive.'

'Well, it was still very odd,' said Molly. 'The old man seemed really nice though, he was a lot like the Wizard from the Magic Council, but not quite as stern looking.'

'Come on, Molly, it's time we were getting back,' called Mr Miggins. He turned away and began to walk back towards the village.

As Molly stepped out of the circle a strong breeze came out of nowhere and blew her thick, curly hair across her face; the wind died abruptly when she took another step away. She looked back towards the circle with a smile on her face. 'Thank you for the food,' she whispered.

Chapter Six

After tea, everyone sat around the dining table swapping stories about famous witches. Granny Whitewand and Great Aunt Willow even managed to argue about the witches who were involved in the tales, even if it was a famous story from the history books that everyone knew. Then they argued about whether to have Cocoa or Hot Chocolate for a bedtime drink, even though neither of them wanted any.

Molly went to bed at nine. She was grateful to hear that Aunt Willow had set up a camp bed in the lounge and Granny Whitewand was going to sleep on that so her snoring didn't keep everyone in the house awake all night. Molly was tired after the travelling and the fresh sea-air and fell instantly asleep. She was woken at exactly midnight when the church bells in the next village rang out the hour. Molly suddenly felt wide awake, she got out of bed, sipped some of the water in the glass at the side of her bed, then walked over to the window and looked out into the night.

A full moon was making its slow way across the sky, creating creepy shadows over the village. Molly stretched her neck to see if she could see what was on the other side of a tall hedge that ran across the field at the back. Then she heard the noise.

It was a stifled sound, not quite a screech and not quite a wail. Molly opened the window and stuck her head out into the night. She was just telling herself that she must have imagined it, when the sound came again, a soft, high-pitched wailing sort of noise. Molly had never heard anything quite like it. She knew the noises that owls and other creatures of the night made, as she'd studied them at the Witch's Academy. This was a weird sound, almost human, but there was something more, something unearthly in there too. Molly ran across to the door where she'd hung her cloak and pulled Wonky from the secret pocket. Quickly she addressed him and reached out of the window with the wand in her hand.

'What's that sound, Wonky? I can't work out what it is.'

'It's a very strange noise isn't it, Molly Miggins? I have to confess I've never heard anything quite like it either.'

'I think a sound like that needs investigating, don't you, Wonky?'

'I'm not so sure, Molly Miggins,' replied the wand. 'It's probably not a good idea to go wandering about in a strange village in the dead of night.'

Molly thought about it for all of three seconds. She slipped Wonky back into her secret pocket and got dressed in record time. She could hear the sound of Granny Whitewand's epic snoring as soon as she opened her bedroom door. She smiled to herself, knowing that no one would hear her leave the house even if they were lying in bed awake. Her grandma's snores could hide the sound of a wailing fire engine.

Molly crept past the lounge door, tiptoed through the kitchen and quietly slipped the bolts on the back door. She took a quick glance over her shoulder, then stepped outside and closed the door quietly behind her. At the bottom of the garden path she looked both ways to make sure no one was about, then she turned left into the narrow lane and hurried down the main street.

She stopped when she got to the village green. The wailing noise seemed to have stopped too. Molly pulled Wonky from her pocket and addressed him.

'Your hearing is better than mine, Wonky, can you still hear that awful noise?'

Wonky was silent for a few moments. 'Whoever, or whatever was making it, appears to have given up, Molly Miggins. Do you think we should go home now?'

Molly shook her head. 'It might start up again, Wonky, then I'll have to get dressed and sneak out for a second time to investigate it. You know I like to solve puzzles.'

Wonky nodded. He knew only too well.

'While we're out here,' said Molly quietly, 'and while there's no one around, I think it's a good time to take a sneaky peek at Cranberry Cottage. Just a quick look, through the fence.'

Before Wonky could tell her that he didn't think it was a very good idea at all, Molly shoved the wand back into her pocket and set off across the green towards the east side of the village.

Cranberry Cottage was set back, well away from the main road, down a thin, dirty track that had become overgrown because it was so little used. Molly stamped down stinging nettles as she walked. She had finally found the path after walking around the village twice. Woodhenge was a very small place and boasted only five streets, all of which led back to each other. The overgrown track had to lead somewhere and as it obviously hadn't been used recently, Molly felt it was the only viable option.

The track dissected a thick wood which meant the cottage couldn't be seen from the main part of the village at all. The bright full moon that had lit up everything like daylight a few minutes earlier was reduced to a dappled, pale light that cast deep shadows across the path. Molly began to feel a little nervous; she reached into her pocket and pulled out her wand.

'I know you said it wasn't a good idea, Wonky, but, well, here we are anyway. I'm not going to do anything silly, I just want a quick look through the fence then we're off, okay?'

Wonky nodded. 'Be extremely careful, Molly Miggins. Belladonna was as powerful a witch as Morgana in her day. She'll still have some of that power left, wraith or not.'

Molly's peered ahead into the gloom. The wood got thicker and the path was harder to find. After another fifty yards, she was convinced that she had lost it completely.

'Can you see the path, Wonky? I think we're in the woods now.'

'We are, Molly Miggins. Steer to the right, past the hawthorn and you'll find it again.'

Molly edged sideways, tripped on an old tree root and just managed to thrust out both hands to stop herself crashing head first into the trunk of a huge elm tree. She put Wonky between her teeth while she massaged her sore wrist, then she took a deep breath, blew out her cheeks and set off again.

Wonky's advice, as usual, was spot on. As soon as she eased past the hawthorn Molly found herself back on the scruffy, weed-ridden, track. The nettles and brambles hadn't taken hold as well on this section of the path and the wood wasn't as thick, so Molly could see the moon through the thin branches directly overhead and she made good progress. She navigated a winding section of path around a cluster of beeches, and found the tall, iron railings looming up in front of her.

Molly stopped just short of the fence and took a deep breath. The silence was almost deafening. Nothing moved in the wood, even the gentle breeze that had been blowing through the leaves in the upper levels of the trees seemed to have died. On the other side of the fence, the moonlight lit up a series of pretty little flower beds and a neatly clipped shrubbery.

'It looks nicer than our garden at home, Wonky. How is that possible after all these years?'

Wonky sniffed the air. 'Magic,' he said. 'Nothing will ever change in that garden unless the spell is removed.'

The fence was twelve feet high, the iron railings, two inches thick and were set three inches apart.

'Whoever built this didn't even want a cat to get through,' said Molly, more to herself than Wonky.

'They have certainly made a good job of it,' agreed the wand. 'Right, Molly Miggins, you've seen the fence, it's time to go home.'

'Not yet, Wonky,' Molly pleaded. 'I just want a quick look at the house.'

Molly followed the fence around to the left, crunching on many years' worth of dead leaves. She looked through the fence into the shrubs and bushes on the other side as she went. After twenty yards she came across a huge double gate that had a sign on it that read: DANGER! CRANBERRY COTTAGE. KEEP OUT! The gate itself had no less than four, thick, metal link chains securing it. Each chain was held by an enormous padlock. Molly lifted one in her hands.

'I wonder if an unlock spell would–'

'Molly Miggins! NO!' Wonky looked at her sternly. This is not a game. Belladonna is a very dangerous witch. You promised that we'd only come to have a look and you've done that. I can't force you to leave, as you are the one who controls me, but I can give advice and my advice is, leave this alone.'

Molly stepped back. The padlock dropped with a clatter that seemed to echo around the whole wood.

'Oops,' said Molly. 'That made enough noise to wake the dead.'

'Don't even joke about things like that, not here at least,' Wonky glanced nervously at the house.

Molly looked beyond the gate into the grounds. A pretty paved path led between two lines of shrubs to a large, stone-paved square that was littered with wooden planters. Beyond that lay Cranberry Cottage. Molly smiled as she took in the view.

'It's so pretty, Wonky, it looks just like one of those cottages they used to put on the old-fashioned chocolate boxes. I had a Christmas card from my best friend Jenny once that had a house just like this one on it... minus the snow of course. I've always wanted to live somewhere like this. It's beautiful.'

Molly was transfixed by the beauty of the cottage. She could feel the wand's uneasiness and knew that she should really make her way back to Aunt Willow's house, but she found that she couldn't summon up the will to leave such a wonderful place.

Then she saw something move.

She thought she'd imagined it at first. She could easily have been mistaken – it could just be a trick of the light – just a shadow, cast by the moon as it shone across the lead-lined, small-paned window at the front of the house. But then she saw the movement again, in the window on the other side of the porch. Molly narrowed her eyes and peered through the gate.

'I wish I had some binoculars with me,' she whispered to herself.

She suddenly found she didn't need binoculars.

The shadow began to get larger. It started in the small pane at the centre of the window, but grew rapidly until it covered all sixteen panes. Then the shadow began to solidify. Molly's feet seemed glued to the spot. She tried to drag her eyes away but something more powerful than her own will kept them fixed on the window. The ghostly shape grew lank, white hair, a pair of narrow eyes and a hook of a nose. Then a cruel mouth and a long chin were added to the vision. The window flew open and a thin, sinewy arm stretched out. A long, skinny finger with a twisted, broken fingernail made a beckoning motion. Molly tried to concentrate on her wand, but a voice filled her mind, a cruel voice, an insistent voice that shut out all other thoughts.

'Come to me,' it said.

Chapter Seven

Molly held her head in her hands as the voice of Belladonna Blackheart grew louder and more insistent by the second.

'Come to me, we shall be one, come to me,' it repeated over and over.

Molly screwed up her face and tried her best to fight the urge to step towards the gates. She attempted to concentrate on Wonky but every time his fat little face appeared in her mind it was instantly replaced by the wrinkled, hate-filled face of Belladonna. Her black eyes burned into Molly's brain but still Molly resisted. Then the old witch changed tactics, the image of the old, hook-nosed, long-chinned hag was transformed into that of a beautiful, fair-haired woman. The voice became sweeter, calmer, almost melodic. Molly took a hesitant step forward, still fighting to resist the charming, welcoming message that played over and over in her head.

'MILLIE! What are you doing in my dream?' Granny Whitewand's croaky old voice swept into Molly's thoughts.

'I'm sorry, Grandma, I was–'

'Get out of it this minute. I was just about to turn Corinda Codswallop's latest love potion into a cauldron full of sago pudding.'

'Sorry, Grandma. I'll go now,' replied Molly.

As Granny Whitewand's voice faded, Belladonna tried to force her way back into Molly's thoughts, but Wonky was too quick.

'To me, Molly Miggins, to me.'

Wonky's fat, friendly little face suddenly filled Molly's mind. She turned away from the gates and took two stuttering paces towards the wood.

'That's good, Molly Miggins, concentrate on me. Two more steps now.' Wonky's voice was smooth, calm, persuading.

Molly stumbled into the trees, keeping her wand fixed in her thoughts. She leaned with her back to the thick trunk of an oak and took in deep breaths.

'It's okay, Wonky, she's gone. I think her telepathy only works close to the property. Thank goodness for Granny Whitewand, I thought I'd gone under there.'

'Your escape was entirely down to you, Molly Miggins,' said the wand, proudly. 'You sent that message to your grandmother in a time of extreme stress. You used your own telepathic powers to block Belladonna's *Mind Trap*. You've come such a long way since we first met. Belladonna must be wondering what's happened. She would have gained control of most other people's minds. You are a very special young witch.'

Molly smiled and took a series of deep breaths. 'We'd better get home, Wonky. I suddenly feel very, very tired.'

Molly woke up late the next morning with the sun streaming in through the open window. She yawned, stretched, then showered and dressed. When she got downstairs she discovered a bowl of Wheaty Flakes on the table and two slices of toast in the rack. She suddenly felt very hungry and attacked her breakfast with gusto.

She found Aunt Willow in the garden chatting to Mr and Mrs Miggins. Granny Whitewand was asleep in a garden chair, head slumped forward, chin on her chest. Every so often she stirred and wafted away an imaginary bee. She had had problems with bees in her dreams for years.

Molly sat down in a garden recliner and wished everyone a good morning. Great Aunt Willow patted her on the shoulder and told her that they were trying to organise a boat trip to Shingleton on the other side of the bay.

'We could get the bus, but it's much more fun crossing on a boat,' she said.

Molly nodded enthusiastically. She had only been on a boat once and that was when she was under arrest, being transported to an offshore, castle gaol.

'When are we going?' she asked.

'I need to get in touch with Daisy Dollop, she has a boat called Flipper, she hires it out for fishing mostly but she owes me a favour so she might take us out. I'll see if she can do it on Monday morning.'

When the conversation turned to more mundane topics, like the weekly shop, Molly got up and announced that she was going for a walk around the village.

'Keep away from Cranberry Cottage,' said Mrs Miggins and Aunt Willow at the same time.

Molly looked away guiltily as the events of the night before came back to her. 'I'm only going for a walk, you don't have to worry,' she said.

Molly turned left down the lane outside Aunt Willow's house, along the main street and down to the village green. At the centre of the green was a large pond with tall reeds and bulrushes framing its banks. Molly found a bench seat, sat down, took off her hat, placed it at the side of her and leaned back to let the gentle breeze blow across her face.

'Hello, Poor Girl,' said an instantly recognisable voice. 'You told me a lot of fibs. This place isn't the slightest bit interesting.'

Molly groaned. *What on earth was Henrietta doing here?*

'You said there was lots to do, you said there was a wooden Stonehenge, you said there was a scary house, but there's nothing. All there is, is… this!'

Henrietta pointed to the pond. 'You got me here under false pretences, Molly Miggins. I'm going to sue you in court when I get back.'

Molly ignored the threat. 'There is a henge, but it's all rotted away now, there's still magic there though. I went there yesterday and–'

'Boriiiiiiiiiiiiiiiing!' Henrietta wasn't amused.

'How did you get here, anyway?' asked Molly.

'I just happened to mention this place after seeing you the other day, to see if Mum or Dad knew where it was, and it turned out that our cook, Betsy Bindipper, has a sister in the next village, so she knew the area well. She said I could stay with her family for the weekend but I'm not going to; their house is far too small and there are five people living in it already.' She held her nose. 'They aren't the cleanest of people either. They smell of fish.'

'Perhaps they're a fishing family,' said Molly.

'They are, but that's no excuse,' replied Henrietta. 'What's your aunt's house like? I might stay there until my chauffeur comes to pick me up tomorrow.'

Molly snorted. 'You're not staying at my aunt's house, so don't even think about it.'

'Why not?' asked Henrietta. 'Is she smelly too?'

'No, she isn't smelly. There's not enough room, Granny Whitewand is sleeping on a camp bed as it is.'

'I'll have your bed then,' said Henrietta. 'You can sleep on the sofa for one night, can't you?'

'No I can't,' said Molly, flatly.

'Dad will pay,' replied Henrietta as though that would sort everything out. 'Anyway, I've got to stay with you. I telephoned a few minutes ago to tell Dad that's where I'll be. I said I'd text the address over later.'

'You're mad,' said Molly. 'You had better ring again and tell them you made a mistake and you need picking up now.'

'You know that's not going to happen,' said Henrietta. 'Move up, I'll sit with you for a bit.'

Molly sighed and moved along the bench. Henrietta sat down and smoothed down her dress, it was white with a very faint, gold-coloured, floral print. She caught Molly looking.

'Do you like it? I suppose you do, you should too. Daddy got it for me from Harrods the last time we went down to London. It's a Zeppo Zodiac original.'

'You mean they only made one dress? That seems a bit silly.'

'No, they didn't make just the one, there were a few of them, it's Zeppo designer wear though, exclusive to Harrods.'

'So, it's not really original, is it?' said Molly. She gave Henrietta the sweetest smile she could muster.

Henrietta scowled. 'It's better than anything you've got. I never see you in anything but that witch's costume.'

'That's… because… I'm… a… witch,' Molly replied as slowly as she could.

Henrietta looked around the village green.

'So, where's this creepy cottage then? The scariest place on the planet.'

'I didn't say that,' said Molly. 'It is a scary place though.'

Henrietta held her hands out, palms up and raised her eyebrows.

'So, where is it?' She looked around again. 'I don't feel very scared; I have to say.'

Molly got to her feet. 'Well, I'd better get back. Aunt Willow is organising a boat trip, it might be this afternoon.'

Henrietta stood directly in front of Molly. 'Where… is… this… scary… cottage?' she demanded to know. 'I bet it doesn't even exist. I bet it's just an ordinary run down cottage, like the rest of them in this dreadful village.'

'I'm not telling you, Henrietta,' said Molly. 'It's far too dangerous for the likes of you.'

She turned away, walked around the seat and headed back towards Great Aunt Willow's cottage. When she reached the garden path she found that Henrietta had been following her.

'Is this it?' Henrietta screwed up her face as she looked at it. 'I suppose it will have to do, at least it doesn't smell of fish.' She noted the house number from the gate and texted a message from her phone.

'3 Lazy Daisy Lane, Woodhenge.'

'Do you know the post code?' she asked. 'For the chauffeur's Sat-Nav thingy.'

'No,' replied Molly.

'Oh well, he'll find it I suppose.' Henrietta looked around. You couldn't get lost in this place if you tried.'

She followed Molly around to the back garden where Great Aunt Willow was pouring tea out of a china pot.

'Hello, Molly. Have you found yourself a little friend already?' she asked with a smile.

Granny Whitewand looked at Henrietta from under the brim of her witch's hat.

'It's that posh girl from the big house, isn't it? What's she doing here?'

'She, er...' Molly didn't know where to start.

'I've come to see this supposedly, scary, haunted house; Cranberry Cottage is it? I'm beginning to have my doubts that it exists at all though. I think Molly has been telling fibs.'

'Oh it exists all right,' said Granny Whitewand.

'You don't want to go there,' added Great Aunt Willow. 'You'll ruin that pretty little dress of yours.'

'WHERE IS IT?' Henrietta stamped her foot. 'I WANT TO SEE IT. TAKE ME THERE THIS MINUTE!'

'You wouldn't get me anywhere near it and I wouldn't encourage anyone else to go there either.' Granny Whitewand struggled to her feet; her knees popped like Champagne corks. 'But, seeing as it's you...'

'No, don't tell her, Grandma,' said Molly quickly.

'It's over there, Granny Whitewand pointed in the vague direction of the village. Just walk around until you see an overgrown track heading off on its own. It's on the same side as the bus stop, about a couple of hundred yards further on. You can't miss it. Bye.'

Granny Whitewand plonked herself down into her seat and picked up her mug of tea. She took a huge slurp and glared at Henrietta. 'Are you still here?' she asked.

Henrietta punched the air. 'Yes,' she said, and turned on her heel. 'I'll be back in time for tea... you're not having fish, are you?' She skipped out of the garden towards Lazy Daisy Lane. 'See you. Wouldn't want to be you,' she called over her shoulder.

'GRANDMA!' Molly was aghast.

'Well, she deserves a fright. Coming here, all cock-sure of herself. I really don't like that girl.' Granny Whitewand put her mug down and leaned back in her chair.

'Nobody likes her,' said Molly, 'but that doesn't mean she should be sent into danger like that. Belladonna watches those gates; Henrietta will have no chance if she uses her *Mind Trap*.'

Granny Whitewand pushed her hat back and turned her eyes to Molly. 'And just how do you know Belladonna's set a *Mind Trap* at the gates, young lady?'

Molly decided not to answer, she turned and ran down the garden after Henrietta. 'I've got to stop her before she finds the path. We may never see her again if I don't.'

Chapter Eight

By the time Molly got onto Lazy Daisy Lane, Henrietta had turned the corner and was nowhere in sight. Molly put on a spurt and ran as fast as she could through the village. Running wasn't her thing though, Henrietta always beat her at sports day at school. She caught a glimpse of her white dress as she turned onto the overgrown track that led to Cranberry Cottage. Molly slowed to a walk to get her breath back.

'Bother,' she said aloud. 'I should have grabbed Aunt Willow's broom.'

She thought about going back for it but decided against. *It would probably cost even more time.*

Molly began to run again and turned into the path a good ninety seconds behind Henrietta. She pulled out her wand as she ran.

'Wonky,' she gasped. 'Henrietta's here, she's heading for the cottage, is there anything we can do to stop her?'

'If she's not in line of sight, we can't really do anything, Molly Miggins. Our only hope is that Belladonna's *Mind Trap* isn't as active during the day.'

'Henrietta would go under in two seconds flat,' panted Molly. She put on another spurt and slapped her arm as it rubbed against a stinging nettle that grew across the path.

As she neared the fence, Molly took a short cut through the wood to try to cut off a corner and make up a few seconds on Henrietta. She came out of the trees just in time to see the four padlocks snap open and the thick, heavy chains clank to the floor.

'Henrietta,' she screamed. 'Stop there, WAIT!'

If Henrietta heard she didn't reply. Instead, she stared fixedly ahead and walked through the gap that had appeared in the gates. Molly leapt forward, pointed Wonky at her and fired a *Release,* spell. Henrietta's pace slowed, she turned around slowly to face Molly.

'Help me,' she whispered.

Before Molly could reply, Henrietta's faced formed a scowl and her voice changed to a crackly croak.

'Stay away, meddler. I have what I want now. Just remember the curse that lies upon this house. If you want to spend the rest of your days running from Morgana, then feel free to follow, otherwise, mind your own business. Go home.'

Henrietta turned back towards Cranberry Cottage and began a slow, zombie-like trudge up the path.

Molly moved towards the gates but as she did, they closed together with a loud clunk. The chains floated up as though they were as light as air and the four padlocks snapped back into place.

Molly grabbed one of the locks and pointed Wonky at the keyhole.

'I won't warn you again,' said a voice in her head.

Molly screwed up her eyes and fired an *Unlock* spell. It missed the padlock and spluttered out in a cloud of yellow smoke.

'Bother, bother, bother, bother,' said Molly. She raised her wand and aimed it at the lock again. This time the spell hit, dead centre; the padlock shook but remained locked.

'There's an extra spell here, Molly Miggins,' said Wonky. 'I can work it out but it will take a little time.'

'We don't have time, Wonky. Henrietta's almost at the door.'

'Move over, Millie, incoming broomstick,' croaked a familiar voice.

Molly leapt out of the way as Granny Whitewand shot through a gap in the trees; she missed Molly by a fraction and crashed into the iron gates.

Molly helped her to her feet as Aunt Willow and Molly's parents ran, panting, out of the wood.

'Are we too late?' puffed Great Aunt Willow.

As if to answer, the front door of Cranberry Cottage opened, and Henrietta Havelots, walked inside.

Chapter Nine

'What are we going to do now?' Molly stared helplessly through the gates as the front door to the cottage closed and Henrietta vanished from view.

'There's not a lot we can do,' said Granny Whitewand. 'It's her own silly fault anyway; she was warned.'

'We can't just leave her in there,' said Molly. 'Her dad's sending the driver to pick her up from Aunt Willow's house tomorrow, she told him she's staying with us.'

'Well it serves her right twice over for telling fibs then.' Granny Whitewand picked up Aunt Willow's broom and straightened a few bent twigs. 'Not a bad broom this, Willow, to say you made it.'

'It's better than any of your old wrecks,' Willow replied.

'THIS IS NO TIME FOR PETTY SQUABBLES!' shouted Molly. 'We have to get Henrietta out of there.'

'I would think she's okay for now,' said Mrs Miggins. She was a High Witch at the academy and had studied wraiths. 'If Belladonna is going to try to boost her energy using Henrietta, it will be tonight. Wraiths don't have much in the way of power during the daylight hours. Henrietta is just under the *Mind Trap* spell for the moment. We've got a few hours to plan.'

'One thing is for sure, we can't just walk up to the front door and ask if we can have our posh girl back,' said Granny Whitewand.

Molly gave her a look. Granny Whitewand rolled her eyes upwards.

'A wraith's power, such as it is, is much stronger at night, and stronger still at a full moon,' continued the High Witch. 'Sadly, we have a full moon tonight.'

'It makes it difficult to sneak in,' said Molly. 'When I was here last night I could see…'

Molly's voice trailed off as all eyes were turned to her.

'I only came for a look; I didn't intend going in.'

'You were told to stay away, Molly. You promised us you would,' Mr Miggins wasn't happy.

'I know, Dad, but… well, you know me and puzzles, I can't resist them.'

'Puzzles are one thing, Molly. Dangerous wraith-witches are something else entirely. That could be you in there now.' Mr Miggins shook his head. 'It doesn't bear thinking about.'

Molly pulled a face. 'But she didn't control me, Dad, she couldn't. I managed to fight her off, didn't I, Wonky?'

The wand nodded. 'It was a very close run thing, but Molly Miggins did manage to get out of Belladonna's *Mind Trap*.'

'You beat a tenth level, High Witch's *Mind Trap*?' Great Aunt Willow's mouth gaped open. 'Molly, you are a continual source of amazement.'

'Molly Miggins has more power than she realises,' said Wonky. 'She is up there with the best, she just needs to believe in herself a little more. I can feel it when she wields me. She is getting stronger by the day and her willpower has to be felt to be believed.'

'She's a chip off the old block is our Millie,' said Granny Whitewand proudly. She leaned forward stiffly and planted a wet, wobbly-toothed kiss on Molly's cheek.

'Urgh,' said Molly, wiping her face on her sleeve.

'I think we should all go home now, get something to eat and make a plan,' said Aunt Willow. 'The best plans are laid on a full stomach, besides which, I think we should have a conference call with a certain wizard. Let's see what he can come up with.'

Molly reluctantly followed the others back through the trees. When they reached the path, Granny Whitewand flew on ahead to, 'put the kettle on.' When the rest of them reached home, they found her in one of the wing-backed chairs in the sitting room, fast asleep. The kettle had almost boiled dry.

Lunch consisted of sandwiches, packets of crisps and slices of Great Aunt Willow's various cakes, which were always delicious.

'This is a bit crumbly for my tastes,' said Granny Whitewand as she pushed a huge chunk of Victoria sponge into her mouth.

'Well, leave it if you don't like it,' replied Aunt Willow, 'no one is forcing you to eat it.'

'I'm just saying, I'd have used an extra egg. When I make cakes I–'

'You *NEVER* make cakes,' replied Aunt Willow, 'and we all know why. You set the school kitchen alight the last time you tried, and that was goodness knows how long ago – we were kids then.'

Granny Whitewand cackled. 'I added a spell to the cake mix to make sure it didn't go flat. It rose all right; it filled the whole oven and then blew the door off. Happy days,' she said.

After lunch, Aunt Willow made more tea and the family went to the sitting room to drink it. Molly took up her usual position on a cushion by the door. After a bit of idle chit-chat, Aunt Willow pulled her wand from her secret pocket and pointed it to the corner of the room.

'*Conference,*' she called.

A pale blue spell floated from the end of Willow's wand and formed a large, misty ball in the corner of the room. The spell swirled around for a while, then a witch's face appeared from the haze.

'Hello, caller. This is the telepathy exchange, who do you wish to speak to?'

'The Wizard from the Magic Council, please,' said Great Aunt Willow.

'One moment caller, I'll see if he's available.'

The witch disappeared; there was a click, then a muffled conversation before she appeared again.

'I'm connecting you now. Have a nice day.'

The mist began to swirl until it formed a foggy shape, the shape became more defined, first a dark blue robe came into view, then a long white beard and a tall, black, pointy hat decorated with yellow stars, then the Wizard's face appeared. The whole form faded and returned twice before finally, full contact was made.

'Hello, Willow, I hope this is important, I've been pulled out of a meeting to take this call.'

The Wizard looked around the room, nodded to Mr Miggins, smiled and bowed to Mrs Miggins and Granny Whitewand then settled his eyes on Molly.

'Hello, Molly Miggins. I was going to get in touch with you soon. I have a new task for you.'

'Thanks,' said Molly, without a lot of enthusiasm, 'but I've got enough on my plate at the moment.'

The Wizard tutted. 'Have you indeed. You might like this task. It could be a lot of fun.'

Molly bit her lip. Her idea of fun and the Wizard's idea of fun were two completely different things.

'I'll see you when I get back from holiday,' she said.

'I will look forward to it, Molly Miggins,' he replied.

The Wizard turned his attention back to Willow.

'So, what is so important that I need to be summoned to a conference call?'

'Belladonna Blackheart,' said Aunt Willow and Granny Whitewand, together.

The Wizard's eyebrows raised.

'Oh dear,' he said. 'It's been a while since I heard that name mentioned. I was hoping it was going to be a lot longer before I heard it again. What's happened?'

'Henrietta Havelots has happened,' said Molly.

'The stupid girl's only gone and fallen into Belladonna's *Mind Trap*,' said Granny Whitewand. She's a pain in the neck, that girl. It would serve her right if we just left her there.'

'Henrietta? What is she doing at Cranberry Cottage? How did this happen?'

Molly held up her hand. 'It's my fault. She was boasting about all the places she's been to and I said, I bet you've never been to Woodhenge. She hadn't, and I was coming here, so I tried to make out it was more interesting than it actually is. I told her about the curse of Cranberry Cottage. You know what Henrietta's like, she can't bear someone to go somewhere she's never visited, so she got her driver to bring her over. She was supposed to be staying with her cook's relatives, but she didn't like it there, she said they all stank of fish, so she decided to stay with us instead. She wasn't invited or anything.'

'It's not entirely Molly's fault,' said Granny Whitewand. 'I must take a teensy-weensy bit of blame too.'

'A teensy-weensy bit?' Molly's mouth dropped open.

The Wizard's eyes settled on Granny Whitewand.

The old witch looked away from the Wizard's piercing gaze. 'All right, I *MIGHT* have told her where to find Cranberry Cottage, but that doesn't mean it's my fault if the silly girl decides to go there, does it?'

The hologram wizard sat down and sighed. 'Right, he said. Tell me everything that's happened, right from the start.'

When they had finished retelling the story, including the bits from Molly about her own adventure at the gates of Cranberry Cottage, the Wizard sat silently for a while, deep in thought. Aunt Willow went to the kitchen to make more tea. When she returned, the Wizard spoke.

'This is very disturbing but also very interesting news,' he began. 'Firstly, we have learned that Belladonna Blackheart still harbours a desire to come back into our world. Secondly, we have learned that Molly Miggins' magical powers have developed far beyond what we expected at such a young age, although we all knew she was an exceptional talent. This gives us hope because we know that Molly can resist her, just as she has resisted Morgana in the past. My only concern is that she is still a very inexperienced witch and she makes hasty decisions sometimes. She will need help with this task.'

The Wizard paused, then continued.

'When I say, help, I don't mean that you should all attack Cranberry Cottage as a group; that just wouldn't work. Belladonna would put up extra spell barriers and it might take us weeks to get past her defences. What we need is a little bit of subtlety, a bit of craftiness. We need to do things that she won't expect us to do. Belladonna is a wraith-witch and she's not as powerful as she was before she entered wraith form, but, if she takes energy from Henrietta, she'll still be a force to be reckoned with. In the first instance, we need to find out what her plans are. It may be that she merely intends to use Henrietta's life force to give her enough power to finish off whatever it was she started all those years ago. We assume she was working to forge a new exit from The Void so that Morgana could return. On the other hand, being the clever, deceitful witch she is… was… it could be that she has a more personal agenda and we may be able to tempt her out of Cranberry Cottage. I think that would be our best hope of defeating her; we have to get her out of her comfort zone and into the open air. That may be a difficult task, but I'm pretty certain she must be fed up with the confines of the cottage by now.'

'I still think we should just kick the door down and blast her with *Fireball* spells until she's a quivering lump of jelly,' said Granny Whitewand. 'Surely she can't fight us all off at once?'

'Too many witches spoil the spell, Hazel Whitewand,' said the Wizard. 'One small, seemingly insignificant witch, could succeed, where many, experienced witches might end up getting in each other's way. We don't want a mass of spells bouncing all over the place, it could make things even more dangerous. No, what we need is a distraction. Just a small one, something to get the attention of the *Mind Spell*, while one, agile, witch sneaks past, unnoticed. Our main weapon is Molly Miggins. Belladonna, like most of you, is from the old school of magic. Molly is from the new school. We teach things in different ways now. Molly has spells that Belladonna has never heard of and she'd have to spend time working out how to respond to them. On top of that, Molly is a young witch, and young witches think in a different way to older ones. Their minds are quicker, more imaginative, and don't forget this; Molly has done something that none of you – great witches that you are – have ever done. She has thwarted Morgana, the most powerful witch the world has ever seen, and she's done it more than once.'

The Wizard paused to let his statement sink in. When he spoke again his voice was calm and reassuring.

'Belladonna thinks in exactly the same way that Morgana thinks. They were from the same time; she would have been head of the Black Academy had Morgana not seized control when she did. She is every bit as arrogant, devious and cruel as Morgana, and that is her main weakness. We have to get under her skin, we have to irritate her, force her into mistakes. We have to use tactics she wouldn't consider using herself. At some point in the future, Molly Miggins will face the severest test of all; we all know this. One day, Morgana and her followers will find a way out of The Void and we have to make sure Molly is ready to face her. The more Molly learns now, the stronger she will become. She needs to learn how the Black Academy witches think, how they react, which spells they'll use and which ones will hurt them in return. Don't forget, their thought processes won't have changed in four hundred years. They won't have moved on as we all have.'

The Wizard paused and gathered his thoughts.

'Because Belladonna is only a wraith-witch it gives us the edge. She will only be able to utilise her full power at night. She'll use Henrietta to attain that power. Somehow, Molly has to find a way into her domain and put an end to Belladonna's plans once and for all. It is high time the curse of Cranberry Cottage was lifted.'

Chapter Ten

The room fell silent. All eyes turned to Molly.

'I don't like it,' said Mr Miggins. 'It's too dangerous. I know we have to do something, but we should think again. There has to be another way.'

'I'm not so sure,' said Aunt Willow. 'We can always attack in force if Molly gets stuck. She has wonderful powers of telepathy. She can let us know if she's in trouble.'

Granny Whitewand scratched her head. 'How about we try it this way? We cause a distraction to allow Molly time to get into the place, then she blocks Belladonna's defensive spells from the inside. Once she's done that, we attack and make mincemeat out of her.' The old witch pulled her white, ash wand from her pocket. 'It's been ages since I fired a good *Thunderbolt*.'

'That sounds more like what I have in mind,' said the Wizard. 'We will have to play things by ear though. We don't know what Molly will find when she gets in there. There may be endless illusory spells floating about the place. We don't know whether Belladonna is in the actual cottage or has some cellar underneath. Molly will need to have her wits about her.'

'What about this curse, though?' Molly frowned. 'I don't really fancy the idea of being sent to The Void so I have to run from Morgana for the rest of my life.'

'The curse is the first thing that has to be removed,' said the Wizard. 'Curses are flimsy bits of magic, easily undone with the right words.'

'Do we know the right words?' asked Molly.

The Wizard shook his head.

'Not yet, but we'll work on it and try to find an answer before you go in, Molly. We have records in our archives that date back to that time. We don't have a lot, but there are some old spell scrolls that Belladonna may have used, in part at least, to set the curse. If my memory serves me correctly, we also have some witness statements that have been handed down in story form. The stories will have been corrupted, like Chinese Whispers over the years, but the basic facts will still be there.'

'Fairy tales? We can't base Molly's plans on stories. We have to give her more to work with than that,' said Mr Miggins who still wasn't happy about things.

'There were over twenty witnesses on the night the curse was cast,' said the Wizard. 'The villagers went to Cranberry Cottage with hate in their hearts, they were fed up of Belladonna's attacks on their livestock and crops; they meant to burn the place down. They didn't because the curse, and the protective magic, were put in place as they attacked. People heard her exact words. We need to piece together the scraps of information we have at our disposal. The answer is there and we'll find it. I'll order Ramona Rustbucket to raid the archives in a few minutes' time. The entire academy staff will turn their thoughts to this problem. I guarantee you'll have the answer before you set off.'

'When will that be?' asked Granny Whitewand with a yawn. 'I need to take forty winks first.'

'You have time for forty winks, Hazel,' replied the Wizard. 'But this job has to be done tonight. I know that Henrietta isn't the most popular person at the moment, but she is a member of our academy.'

'But her father–' Granny Whitewand interjected.

'I am aware that her father pays us a great deal of money by way of fees to keep his daughter in our institution and I'm also aware that she wouldn't make a decent witch in a thousand years, but that doesn't make any difference. She is a member and therefore our sister. It is our duty to find her and rescue her.'

'If Henrietta was my sister, I'd leave home,' Molly muttered.

The Wizard clapped his hands. 'Right, I'll go and find Ramona Rustbucket and we'll get to work. I'll call another conference when we have an answer.'

The mist evaporated in an instant, and the Wizard was gone.

Molly spent the afternoon reading Great Aunt Willow's copy of The Witcher. She was particularly interested in the section on wraith-witches.

"Wraith-witches are apparitions that appear just before death. A spell is cast in the last few seconds of life, and the witch's image is created. This state differs from ghosts in that the wraith is still partly alive. Powers of wraith-

witches are often limited. During the daylight hours they are severely restricted and they must stay out of direct sunlight or the wraith spell will be undone and the last bit of the witch-spirit will pass over. During the hours of darkness, the wraith-witch can be much more active. Should they gain access to a life source, their powers will increase substantially, (this power, though slightly limited, can last into the daylight hours if the wraith-witch is in continual shadow or completely cut off from the sun's rays.) Wraiths are listed as a category 4 on the danger scale. This increases to category 9 if a life source is available for the-wraith-witch to tap energy from."

'Bother,' said Molly, who was getting a little frustrated about having to wait until nightfall before she could make a start on her task. After reading how wraith-witches function and knowing that Belladonna had a life force to provide energy, she had hoped that the Wizard would get back to them with plenty of daylight hours left; Belladonna would be at her weakest then. Molly suspected that she would have more than a few surprises in store whatever time she entered the cottage.

The call finally came through at 7.30pm. Molly had almost given up and was trying to formulate a plan that would allow her to sneak into the cottage, unnoticed. She had a long conversation with Wonky about *Protect and Defend* spells.

Aunt Willow called everyone into the lounge when the call came in. They stood around the coffee table as the apparition in the corner took shape.

'Hello, everyone,' the Wizard began. 'Firstly I'd like to tell you all that we think we have most of the words that Belladonna used the night she set the curse. It took us a little longer than we thought, because some of the witness statements mixed up the curse and the protection spell that she put on the cottage and gardens. I'll come to the *Protect* spell, later, as we are not going to try to damage the property in any way... not yet at least. I will translate from the language of the time and replace any 'prithees, anons and troths with a modern interpretation of what was said.'

The Wizard picked up a piece of parchment and read from it.

"By the laws of magic, I set this curse. That any person, alive, or as yet unborn, who shall trespass over this threshold, shall be cast into the darkest void, for all eternity."

'So, you see, the curse does not affect those who walk the grounds, which is probably why there were no reports of people going missing over the years, especially the Parish Council workmen who tried unsuccessfully to demolish the place. The curse only affects those who seek to gain access to the building. The *Mind Trap* is a far more recent addition. We believe Belladonna added this and the *Gate Lock* spell when the gardens were fenced off, about fifty years ago.'

'That doesn't help us much, though does it?' said Mr Miggins. He put his arm protectively around Molly's shoulder.

'No, but it does do away with one of the myths that has been allowed to flourish over the years. That's what I meant about Chinese Whispers.' The Wizard looked at his notes and carried on.

'Fiona Fastcaster, our expert on curses and hexes, has looked at some old spell fragments from Belladonna's time and she's assured me that her curse can be removed by the use of a simple *Remove Hex* spell. This is part of the same family of spells as the *Undo* spell you use now, Molly, but it works in a subtly different way, and you have to use the older version of the spell, not the replacement that came in sometime in the 19th century. I'll send you the spell via telepathy in a few moments.'

Molly looked surprised. She wasn't aware that spells could be learned that way.

'Now, regarding the protection spell…' the Wizard again referred to his notes. 'The spell will be active whilst the caster, in this instance, Belladonna, is resident, or within a reasonable distance of the property. This distance can be up to, but not exceeding, five miles. From the snippets of information we have, Belladonna would almost certainly have used a basic *Protect and Defend* spell. There wasn't much else about to protect property in those days, most *Protect* spells, then and now, are used to defend people. So, to remove it, just use your modern, *Undo Protection* spell. It was in your first ever upgrade, Molly, that's how simple a spell it is.'

'I don't want to be rude, but if it's all as easy as this, why couldn't you get past the front door when you tried?' asked Mr Miggins.

'I was coming to that,' said the Wizard tersely.

'It appears that a secondary spell was added to the curse when it was invoked. At the time I wasn't aware of this.' The Wizard lifted his notes again. 'According to one of the witnesses, there may have been three separate spells cast that night. We know the first two, but we have no idea what the third one was. It's obviously a spell to allow access; some sort of password maybe. I was puzzled at the time because I tried numerous *Undo* spells with different combinations, but I couldn't find a way in. I must admit, I didn't try to guess a password. I'm hoping Molly can come up with something herself. She will be safe enough on the threshold of the cottage as the curse only comes into effect when the threshold has been crossed, and anyway, Molly now has the means to remove it.'

The Wizard looked at Molly, fondly.

'So, Molly Miggins. It's down to you now. Are you ready to start the spell transference?'

Molly nodded and stared directly into the eyes of the Wizard. She felt a tingling sensation in the back of her neck, then she heard the Wizard's voice clearly in her mind.

'Good luck, Molly Miggins, if anyone can succeed in this quest, it is you. Remember, just be yourself, don't think about what anyone else would do in the circumstances, this is your task now. You may receive help later, but your first objective will be to remove all the traps and illusions from the inside of Cranberry Cottage, then, hopefully, you will be able to find a way into Belladonna's lair. I'd just like to take a moment to say how immensely proud of you the whole of the academy is. I wish you good fortune, Molly Miggins. I will see you on your return. Goodbye for now.'

The Wizard bowed to each of the witches in turn, then nodded towards Mr Miggins.

'You will all have a part to play before this story is ended. Good luck to each and every one of you.'

The mist cleared, taking the image of the Wizard with it.

Chapter Eleven

At 8.30pm, Molly picked up Great Aunt Willow's spare broom and took it for a test flight. She wanted to get a look at the grounds of the cottage from the air to see if there were any obvious traps set in the garden. To get a feel for the broom she flew down to the sea shore and across the cliff tops. When she was confident with the way the broom reacted to her commands, she took it out across the bay and skimmed the waves for a time before flying back by way of the ancient circle at Woodhenge. She flew around the perimeter of Cranberry Cottage three times before she was satisfied that she had memorised the whole layout.

The cottage itself was in the centre of the property, which had gardens on all four sides. The iron fence at the back of the house butted up against an incredibly steep hill that would have taken a skilled mountain climber some time to traverse. The other three sides were surrounded by woodland. There was a stone building in the back garden of the house, about five yards in from the fence. It had a slate roof and no windows that Molly could see. The only way in or out was via an arch-shaped, metal studded, oak door.

Molly landed in Aunt Willow's front garden, as the sun was just beginning to set.

'How did you find it, Molly?' asked Aunt Willow.

'It handles really nicely, it's very responsive,' replied Molly.

'Not as responsive as one of my brooms, though, hey, Millie?' Granny Whitewand plucked at a few of the twigs at the back end of Molly's borrowed broom. 'The one I made for your Marsh-Witch, friend, Misty, for instance?'

'That was a very special broom, Grandma. But my name is Molly,' said Molly. 'The broom was beautiful. I'd love to have one just like it.'

Granny Whitewand preened as she looked at Willow.

Willow pulled a face at her sister. 'I'll make you one, Molly; you've never seen one of my special brooms, have you? I've won first prizes at the national witch fair with them.'

'Only because I didn't enter,' said Granny Whitewand.

Molly took the broom back from Granny Whitewand and leaned it against the wall.

'Mum, Dad, have you finalised your distraction plan yet? The sun's about to go.'

Mr and Mrs Miggins came out of the kitchen and closed the door behind them.

'We do have a plan that we think will work, Molly,' said Mr Miggins. 'We're going to make out we're about to launch an attack on the gates. Dad will go first as he is a master of telepathy, he uses it in his stage act, as you know. Belladonna won't find him an easy conquest.' She smiled at her husband. 'While she's busy trying to keep him out, I'll try a couple of spells I know won't work, on those padlocks. Belladonna will have to choose which one of us to set her thoughts on. While I'm doing that, Granny Whitewand and Great Aunt Willow will fly back and forth across the gates, just above fence height, as though they're checking out the lie of the land. We're convinced that her *Mind Trap* can't possibly focus on four of us at the same time. If it can, then she's a far more powerful wraith than we've given her credit for.'

Mrs Miggins crouched down in front of Molly. 'Granny Whitewand will send you a telepathic message when we have engaged Belladonna. You seem to be able to communicate very easily with her.'

Granny Whitewand grinned a wobbly-toothed grin. 'Don't go jumping the gun, Millie, wait for me to call.'

'I'll wait, Grandma,' replied Molly. 'But please, don't fall asleep and forget.'

Granny Whitewand cackled. 'Oh, Millie, you are funny. As if I'd do that.'

Molly carried her broom down through the village as she walked with her parents and Great Aunt Willow. Granny Whitewand, whose knees, 'aren't up to overgrown paths, these days', flew along in front. Every so often she doubled back to check on their progress.

'Come on, you lot,' she croaked. 'I'm really looking forward to this, it's ages since I was involved in a bit of subterfuge.'

When they reached the iron-railed fence at the end of the track, Molly said her goodbyes and gave each of them a hug. 'Good luck with the distraction ploy,' she said.

'Remember, don't go in until you get my call, Millie,' said Granny Whitewand.

'It's MOLLY, Grandma,' Molly frowned.

'So you keep telling me,' said the old witch.

Molly watched the four family members walk off towards the gates, then she sat down on an old tree stump and pulled out her wand from her secret pocket.

'Hello, Molly Miggins, are we about to go?' he asked.

'We're just waiting for the signal from Granny Whitewand, Wonky,' Molly replied. 'I hope she can stay awake long enough to send it.'

Ten minutes later, Molly still hadn't heard from her grandmother.

'Should I try to call her instead, Wonky? She might have got hold of the wrong end of the stick as usual and be waiting for me to contact her.'

'Give it another couple of minutes, Molly Miggins. It could be that Belladonna is too busy to use her *Mind Trap*, tonight.'

'Molly tapped her foot impatiently and counted down the seconds. After two minutes, exactly, she lifted her wand, closed her eyes and called up the *Telepathy* spell.

'Granny Whitewand, are you there? Calling Granny Whitewand, are you there?' she chanted.

Molly suddenly found herself in a cluttered room, full of spell scrolls and dusty old books.

Granny Whitewand was sitting in an arm chair in front of a blazing fire with her back to Molly. There was a closed door to the right from behind which came a loud and very monotonous, buzzing sound.

'You were supposed to call me,' said Molly.

'Was I?' said a voice that did not belong to Granny Whitewand. The witch got out of the chair and turned to face Molly.'

Molly gasped as she recognised the face that sneered at her from across the room. She had seen that hooked nose, that cruel mouth and those piercing eyes before; in the window of Cranberry Cottage.

'So, meddler, what have you to say for yourself? You invited me in here after all.' Belladonna looked slightly puzzled. 'You didn't sound like an insignificant, junior witch when we spoke in my *Mind Trap* a few moments ago. You sounded much older.'

Just then, Molly heard the sound of a door slamming and the scraping of boots on a stone floor.

'Get out of my way you pesky bees, I want to get into that room.'

The door burst open and in shuffled Granny Whitewand, followed by upwards of two thousand bees.

'Hello, Millie, what are you doing here?' Granny Whitewand had to shout to make herself heard.

Molly pointed towards the chair where a clearly terrified Belladonna was surrounded by the swarm of bees. 'Call them off, call them off. I hate bees,' she screamed.

Granny Whitewand winked and put her wobbly-toothed mouth next to Molly's ear.

'Off you go, Millie,' she cackled. 'Belladonna will be kept busy here, for a short while at least. She walked right into my trap.'

Chapter Twelve

Molly ended the *Telepathy* spell and leapt to her feet. She straddled the broom and brought Wonky crashing down. '*FLY*,' she cried.

The broom rose into the air and Molly wasted no time on flying etiquette, she brought the wand crashing down on the broom again and again. '*FLY, FLY, FLY*,' she yelled. The broom shot forward at such a pace that Molly was almost thrown off the back. She quickly got control and made for the rear garden of the cottage. She landed the broom neatly behind the vegetable patch, then ran to the back of the building, where she took three deep breaths before sneaking a peek around the corner.

Once she had determined that the path was clear, Molly ran down the side of the house, ducked under two small leaded windows, and parked her broom in a narrow recess, then she tiptoed to the front corner of the cottage.

Down at the front of the property, she could see her family standing by the gates. Granny Whitewand sat with her back to the padlocks, obviously asleep. Molly hoped the bees were still busy. She desperately wanted to call to them, to let them know she was almost at the front door, but she dared not.

Molly took another deep breath and hared across the flagstones towards the front door of the cottage. She ducked under the right-hand-side window and didn't straighten up again until she was in the centre of the doorway. She shivered, the warm night had suddenly turned very cold.

The front door was made of stout oak planks, decorated with two large, black-painted, iron hinges and a black-painted, drop-ring handle. Molly resisted the temptation to twist the handle, and addressed her wand instead.

'Here we are, Wonky, what do we do now?' she asked.

'We try the password spell of course,' replied the wand. 'I doubt it will be a sophisticated spell like we have nowadays, the sort where you only get three guesses before an alarm sounds. If I remember correctly, most password spells were just one word or a simple phrase back in Belladonna's day; it shouldn't be too difficult to work out. Sometimes they just used the word, *Open*.'

'Okay,' said Molly, 'let's start with that.' She pointed Wonky towards the ring-handle of the door. '*Password, Open*,' she whispered.

Nothing happened.

'*Password, Remove*,' said Molly.

Nothing happened.

'*Password, Remove Password*,' she said.

Nothing happened.

'*Password, Unshut*,' said Molly.

The door remained closed.

'*Password, Undo*,' said Molly.

Nothing happened.

'Bother,' said Molly.

'We could try using her name,' said Wonky.

'Good idea,' replied Molly. She aimed the wand again.

'*Password, Belladonna,*' she said.

Nothing happened.

'*Password, Belladonna Blackheart*,' said Molly.

The door stayed shut.

'We'll be here all night at this rate, it could be anyth...'

Molly smiled. 'I think I've got it, Wonky.' She aimed the wand at the door handle again.

'*Password, Morgana*,' she said.

The black ring-handle made a squealing sound, as though it needed oiling, and twisted to the left. The door creaked as it opened.

'WE DID IT WONKY!' cried Molly and stepped forward.

'WAIT! Molly Miggins, don't take a step further.'

Molly stopped dead and looked around, thinking that Wonky had spotted some sort of trap.

'The curse?' said the wand.

'Phew! Thanks for the reminder, Wonky, I'd forgotten all about that. I could be waking up in the darkest reaches of The Void, about now.'

Molly raised her wand and pointed into the darkness of the cottage and tried to remember the spell the Wizard had telepathically sent to her.

'*By the laws of magic, I lift this curse. Remove Hex.*'

Molly wondered if the spell had worked at first, because nothing seemed to happen. Then the air in the space in front of her seemed to become unstable, the temperature dropped, noticeably. Molly shivered and wrapped her cloak tightly around her body. There was a gurgling noise, similar to the sound you hear when the last bit of bathwater goes down the plug hole, then absolute silence.

'Well done, Molly Miggins,' said Wonky, 'that was excellent reasoning.'

'Lucky guess,' said Molly with a grin. She loosened her cloak, took a deep breath, and stepped into the dark hallway of Cranberry Cottage.

Chapter Thirteen

The entrance hall of Cranberry Cottage was pitch black. Even though the front door was still open, not a beam of moonlight could find its way into the house. It was as though an invisible, inch-thick steel curtain had been drawn across the aperture. Molly reached behind, blindly, and gave the door the slightest of pushes. Although the door had creaked open as though it hadn't budged an inch in centuries when it was being unlocked, it slipped back with the ease of a well-oiled bolt when it closed. There was the faintest of clicks, and then total silence.

Molly stood perfectly still and held her breath in case Belladonna has been alerted by her entry. After a full minute, with her ears pricked, listening for the slightest noise, Molly decided that it was safe to try a *Glow In The Dark* spell. The darkness was so complete that as soon as she spoke the words of the spell, the hall appeared to be lit by the beams of twenty, high-powered torches. She quickly scaled back the spell until the glow from the wand had about the same output as a single candle.

The hall was square in shape with dirty, rough-plaster walls and had three, thick-plank timber doors leading from it. Molly tiptoed to the single door on the left hand side and eased it open. Inside she found a large oak chest and a narrow, wooden-framed bed with a small, roughly-made table at the side. On the floor next to the bed was a mat made from dried rushes. On the table was a brown, saucer-sized plate with a small, tallow candle stuck to it. The bed was covered with a tatty-looking, woollen blanket. There was a thick, lumpy bolster across the top end. The mattress made a crackling sound when Molly pressed down on it.

'The mattress and the bolster have been stuffed with straw, Molly Miggins,' said Wonky. 'Only the rich could afford feather beds when this house was built.'

'It smells musty,' said Molly. 'I don't think I could sleep on it.'

'It was better than what the poor people had at the time,' replied Wonky. 'Many people slept on straw on the floor, some even slept in the barn or in the stable with the animals.'

Molly screwed up her nose. 'Belladonna should open a window or two and let some air in.'

'They used to think fresh air was bad for you,' said Wonky, 'they thought baths were too.'

Molly shuddered, 'I don't want to think about how they must have smelled in the summer.' She carefully opened the lid of the oak chest. Inside was another rough blanket, a thick, black, cloak and a roll of dark-coloured cloth.'

She closed the lid of the trunk, crossed the room and stepped out into the hall, closing the door quietly behind her.

'Which door now, Wonky?'

'The door on the right looks interesting, Molly Miggins,' replied the wand.

Molly tiptoed across the hall, lifted the latch handle and pushed the door open. Inside she found a neat sitting room with a rush mat in the centre of the floor. Near the window was an ancient-looking rocking chair. It had no arms, a box style seat, and two thick curved rockers underneath. At the side of the rocking chair was a small, square table, roughly made out of sawn off planks. A book with a faded, animal-skin, cover had been left on it. Molly picked it up and opened the fly leaf.

'The Book of Magicke, Curses and Spells,' she read.

Molly flicked through the book looking for a spell she might recognise, but the writing was almost illegible and not many of the words meant anything to her; the ones that did seemed to have been spelt wrongly.

'They used to write a lot of things as they sounded, back then,' said Wonky and they used an f instead of an s, sometimes.'

Molly put the book down. 'I'm glad I don't have to learn my spells from that book at the academy,' she said.

She looked around the room but there wasn't much else of note; just a couple of balls of wool and some sort of weaving frame.

Molly walked back to the hall and opened the third door. Behind it was the kitchen.

The kitchen was built onto a flagstone floor. Placed at the centre of the room was a huge oak table littered with various cooking pots, dirty crockery and a couple of long, sharp-looking knives. Against one wall was a panelled cupboard with two open shelves built on top. The shelves were stacked with piles of plates and jars of stuff that Belladonna used when cooking. On top of the cupboard section was a wooden tray with a fresh-looking loaf of bread sat on it. The far wall was completely taken up with a wide, inglenook fireplace, where a large, black cooking pot was suspended on two metal link chains over an unlit, log fire. By the side of the fireplace was a wooden pail of what appeared to be freshly drawn water. There was a sleek-looking broom leaning against the wall in the corner. Molly was impressed with the freshness of everything. Belladonna's *Protect* spell obviously worked on the food and water too. Everything was preserved exactly as it was in the moments before she became a wraith.

'This is the last room, Wonky, there's nowhere else to look. There must be a secret door somewhere.'

Molly walked around the four walls of the kitchen looking for any signs of a secret door. She searched under the table and crawled around on her hands and knees checking every individual flagstone, but she found nothing.

'I wonder if there's an attic room?' she said.

Wonky thought about it for as moment. 'There might be, but I doubt it would be the sort of place that Belladonna would hide out in. It seems to me that it would be rather dangerous, lighting a fire to boil your cauldron or test out any sort of heat spell in a roof space. Some of the spell ingredients she stored would be highly inflammable too. I think we should be searching for a cellar, rather than an attic.'

'That makes sense, Wonky, the trouble is, there's no sign of one. I've been over every inch of this floor.'

'Let's try a little *Reveal* spell,' said Wonky. 'That might help.'

Molly held the wand out at arm's length and turned slowly around. '*Reveal,*' she called.

A yellow smoke drifted out of the silver tip of her wand. The smoke thinned as it spread out and rose to ceiling level where it petered out, revealing nothing.

'How odd,' said Molly. 'It shows nothing, yet there must have been a lot of magic cast in this room. There has to be a hidden door somewhere.'

Wonky looked puzzled. 'I'm quite surprised by this too, Molly Miggins, because the *Reveal* spell has been in existence since long before Belladonna's time. It should have shown something. Unless, of course there is nothing hidden in the kitchen.'

Molly sat down on a rickety stool and thought for a few moments.

'There has to be something hidden, Wonky, because we know she's in here somewhere. I saw her face in the front window of the house, and… where is Henrietta? We saw her going in, and she hasn't come out as far as we know.'

'I agree, Molly Miggins,' said Wonky. 'I think we should try a few other spells to see if we can get to the bottom of this.'

Molly sat on the stool and cast a few spells that she hoped would reveal something of Belladonna's hiding place but nothing seemed to work. All the *Unhide* spell did, was to make a pot of poppy seeds move along the shelf to reveal a small wooden spoon that had slipped behind it. The *Show* spell showed nothing at all, whilst the *View All* spell merely sat in the air in a blue haze for thirty seconds before disappearing with a quiet, phut sound.

For once, Wonky was stumped. Then Molly had an idea.

'What about that new spell the Wizard put in the latest spell book, the one without a description? It must do something; I'd like to see what.'

She waved her wand lightly in the air and called '*Replay*'.

At first it appeared that nothing had happened, then a pale-grey spell slid out of Wonky and dispersed into the air. Molly let out a quiet sigh and slumped down onto the stool. Then she spotted something move in front of the fire, there was another movement over by the cupboard and when she looked behind she could see a blurred movement coming through the door from the hall.

'What's going on, Wonky?' asked Molly, 'all this blurry stuff is making my eyes go funny.' She turned around on the stool and watched as the whole kitchen became a mass of ghostly shapes, none of them ever still, each one passing across, or even straight through, another blurry figure's path.

'I think I know what this is, Molly Miggins,' said Wonky.

'Do tell,' said Molly. Her eyes darted from side to side trying to make sense of the quick moving images.

'I think you are looking at all of Belladonna's movements, whenever she spent time in this kitchen,' said Wonky. 'But, because she's been in here many hundreds of times, we can't see any individual movements.'

'So, it's a bit like watching a film that's been recorded hundreds of times, one on top of the other,' said Molly.

'Exactly,' said Wonky. 'All we have to do now is find a way to pick out the individual recordings.'

'I'll try,' said Molly, excitedly. She held Wonky out in front of her.

'*Slow Motion Replay*,' she called.

The blurred movement slowed down but there were still too many figures moving about to make any sense of anything.

'*Oldest Replay First*,' Molly called.

The blurred figures disappeared and Molly was left looking at a middle-aged witch, walking into the kitchen with a pail of water. She set it down by the table, opened a small sack of wheat seed and proceeded to grind it into flour in a stone bowl with the use of a large, smooth pebble.

'Well done, Molly Miggins,' said Wonky. 'This must be Belladonna's first day in the cottage. Shall we move on a bit?'

'*Move on twenty years and Replay*,' said Molly. The figure of Belladonna disappeared from the table and reappeared by the big cooking pot. She dipped in a ladle and tasted what looked like stew.

'Try to get something more recent, Molly Miggins,' said Wonky.

Molly thought for a while, wondering which words to choose, in the end she decided on *Latest Replay*'.

Molly looked around the empty kitchen. 'I don't think that one worked, Wonky…'

Molly's voice tailed off as Henrietta Havelots strolled into the room. Her eyes were fixed on the inglenook fireplace. She walked across the kitchen and stood in front of the huge, black cooking pot, then she reached out her hands, took hold of the chains and pulled down hard. There was a grating noise and the flagstone to the right of the fireplace slid across, leaving a black space. Henrietta stepped into the hole and began to descend. Thirty seconds later the slab slid back and the chains holding the cooking pot rattled into place.

'Found it,' said Molly. She leapt off her stool and ran to the fireplace. She put Wonky between her teeth, took hold of the thick chains and pulled down with all her might. The flagstone to the right of the fireplace slid back, Molly took Wonky in her right hand, held him over the dark space and brightened the *Glow in the Dark* spell a little. Below, she could see a set of very worn stone steps. She took one last look around the kitchen, plucked up all of her courage, held Wonky in front of her and began the descent into the darkness.

Chapter Fourteen

The steps were steep and narrow. Molly's feet hung over the edge as she descended. She put one hand on the stone wall and leaned back slightly to try to ease her fear of falling. Large, beautifully woven cobwebs hung in the space above her head. After a dozen steps the stair took a sharp left turn. Molly hesitated before she rounded the corner, and listened for any sound from the cellar but all was quiet.

Around the turn, the incline was less steep and she found that she could look down without feeling nauseous. The stairway came out into a low, brick-lined passage. Molly had to take off her hat and stoop slightly in able to walk along it.

'This Belladonna must be very short, Wonky,' she whispered. 'I'm only five feet and I'm having to stoop.'

'She's an old witch, Molly Miggins; people in Belladonna's time weren't all that much smaller than they are today, one or two inches at most. It's a bit of a myth that they were. The tunnel was probably built this size to save money, time and effort.'

The tunnel was thankfully short, and a few paces later she was able to straighten up as she stepped into what looked to be a store room. There were rough-plank shelves on the wall carrying pots and jars. The left hand wall was lined with wooden barrels.

'I wonder what's in those,' whispered Molly. 'It might be gunpowder or something.'

'I doubt that, Molly Miggins,' replied Wonky. 'They are more likely to be full of apples or salted fish. If they contain liquid, then it's probably weak beer. They couldn't trust the water back then, a lot of it was contaminated. Plague was a regular visitor to the towns around here. So, they drank very weak beer, because the water was cleansed of bugs during the brewing process.'

'You're a mine of information, Wonky,' Molly grinned. 'I'm taking you with me the next time I have a history test.'

There were two, low-arched exits from the store room. One led to another short passageway with a locked door at the end. Molly tiptoed back the way she had come and tried the other exit.

She found herself in a witch's stockroom. The walls were lined with jars of spell ingredients. Molly saw pots of spider's legs, bats wings, toad's eyes, and there was even a short, green, snakeskin hanging from a hook in the corner. In the centre of the room was an enormous cauldron, balanced on a rusty iron frame, above an unlit, log fire. On a plank bench below the jars of spell-making materials, was a selection of scrolls. Molly picked one up and looked at it, but it was written in the same style as the spell book upstairs and she couldn't make head nor tail of it. She tried another scroll. This one contained a childlike drawing of a group of witches walking through a tunnel. At the end of the tunnel, standing in an opening was a witch holding a wand aloft. Underneath the line of witches were the words, Morgana, and Void. Belladonna's name was written under the single witch. Another scroll had a drawing of a young girl sitting in a cage while a bent, old witch cast a spell over her. The spell name was written underneath but Molly couldn't read it.

'This is ancient magic, Molly, it translates to something like, "Drain Life Force". It basically means drawing the energy from a younger person to give vitality to an old one.'

'That's disgusting,' said Molly. She sighed deeply. 'I suppose that's exactly what she wanted Henrietta for.'

'And you, Molly Miggins. Don't forget, she tried to lure you in first.'

A scuttling noise came from behind. Molly swept around, her wand ready to strike. In the corner of the room, a small, brown rat sat on its haunches and cleaned its whiskers.

Molly let out a sigh of relief. 'I wonder how old that rat is? It could be a modern day rat, or it could be a seventeenth-century one. She pushed herself back against the bench and pointed Wonky at the rodent. 'They carried the plague didn't they?'

'Some of them did, not all, and they were thought to be the black variety. That one is brown, and because he's not the least bit scared of us, I'd say that this particular rodent could well be Belladonna's pet. There's plenty of fresh food for it to live on. Nothing ever goes rotten down here.'

Molly gave the rat one last, nervous look and walked out of Belladonna's workshop. She retraced her steps until she came to the short passageway with the locked door at the end.

'I suppose this is where she'll be then, Wonky,' said Molly with just the slightest tremor in her voice.

'It appears to be the only option, Molly Miggins,' agreed the wand.

'Right,' said Molly. She stood with her feet about eighteen inches apart, balanced herself and got ready to fire a follow up *Thunderbolt* if she was attacked after casting her *Unlock* spell.

Molly blew out her cheeks, then expelled the air. She pointed Wonky at the iron-ring handle and called, '*Unlock.*'

A magenta coloured spell eased out of her wand and hit the iron ring where it was nailed to the door. There was a faint, almost inaudible click. Molly stepped forward and twisted the handle. The door opened silently. Molly pushed Wonky out in front of her and stepped inside.

The room was well lit; at least ten candles flickered in the gentle movement of air that Molly caused when she opened the door. Directly ahead of her was another plain, wooden door. To her left, just behind the door she had just opened were two large, domed cages suspended from the ceiling on single, thick chains. One cage was empty, its door hung open as if awaiting the return of a huge canary. Inside the other cage, squatting on her haunches, was a wrinkled old hag. Her long white hair hung in rat's tails down the sides of a thin, age-lined face. Her eyes were fixed onto a pair of bony hands that rested on an even bonier pair of knees. The hag's dress was white, with just a very faint, gold-coloured, floral pattern running through it. Molly recognised it immediately.

'Henrietta! Oh my goodness, what has she done to you?'

Chapter Fifteen

'I've borrowed some of her life force for a while, that's what I've done to her,' said a sweet, soft voice.

Molly spun around on her heel and brought Wonky up from her side, but the blast of a sharp *Thunderbolt* spell knocked it from her hands.

Belladonna Blackheart smiled. 'You won't be needing that for a while.' A brown boot appeared from beneath her thick, black skirt and she kicked Wonky across the floor out of Molly's reach. The wand rolled underneath a pile of firewood and disappeared from view.

Molly looked from the pile of firewood back to Belladonna. She was nothing like Molly imagined her to be. She was pale-skinned and very pretty. She had a dimpled chin, and the deepest of blue eyes. Her long blonde hair hung in waves around her shoulders. The black tunic, skirt, and cloak emphasised the paleness of her skin. Molly could see little bits of Henrietta in her looks.

'Pretty, aren't I?' Belladonna's giggle sounded a lot like Henrietta's.

'It's not fair, what you've done to Henrietta,' said Molly.

'I don't suppose it is... fair, but who cares? I certainly don't.' Belladonna giggled again.

Molly was surprised, she had expected Belladonna to speak in some old fashioned kind of English, but she could have been listening to one of her friends at school. Belladonna seemed to pick up on what Molly was thinking.

'The words and phrases I'm using are quite unfamiliar to me, but it's all part of the package.' She pointed to Henrietta's cage with a long, elegant finger. 'I get her vocabulary as well as her youth. That's a win, win situation, I'd say.' She smiled at Molly again and put a soft hand on her shoulder.

'Come with me. You and I are going to have a nice long chat. It's been so long since I had a proper conversation.' She looked back over her shoulder at Henrietta. 'Sadly, she wasn't in the mood, or the condition, for a girly chat.'

She led Molly across the room to where a pair of barrels sat, side by side. She took a thick, hessian-sack from a pile at the side and dropped it over the top of the barrels. 'There, now we'll be nice and comfy,' she said.

Molly flicked a quick glance to the woodpile where Wonky lay hidden.

'Oh, forget about your silly wand,' said Belladonna. 'It was a very old, twisted little thing. What went wrong, couldn't they find you a new one at the academy?'

Molly was about to argue that Wonky wasn't just any battered old wand, but she held her tongue and said nothing. The less Belladonna knew about her, the better.

Belladonna swivelled around on her barrel and crossed her legs. She looked Molly up and down.

'So, you're the new breed of witch, are you? I can't say I'm all that impressed. That one over there is even less impressive. I read her mind for a while earlier on, just for something to do. There wasn't a lot going on in there I have to say, although she does think rather a lot of herself.'

Belladonna brushed a bit of straw off her skirt and continued.

'Do you know, I almost burst out laughing when I realised she was a White Academy witch. Honestly, if she's the best they can come up with then Morgana is going to have a nice, easy time taking over when she gets back.' She looked Molly up and down again. 'And you, junior witch, who are you, what level have you attained?'

Molly decided to lie.

'I've only just joined. My Grandma was a witch so they let me in; they're short of numbers these days.'

'Oh dear,' Belladonna was full of sympathy. 'So, you haven't even got to level one yet? That's a shame. To add insult to injury, they lumber you with a sad bit of old wood and call it a wand. Poor you.'

'Henrietta's my senior,' said Molly. 'I want to be as good as her one day.'

Belladonna laughed her sweet laugh. 'Aim higher, my dear. She'll never make a witch in a year of Sunday's let alone a month's worth.' She put her wand on her lap and nodded towards it. 'This is Stinger; he's a very old wand. Isn't he gorgeous? I'd let you hold him but, well, I wouldn't want you to try anything silly like throw it away.' She smiled again. 'What's your name anyway? I'm Belladonna, but I think you already know that.'

'I'm Molly Miggins,' said Molly.

'So, Molly Miggins, what are you doing here?'

'I came to get Henrietta back, the Wizard from the Magic Council said I had to because she's my senior witch.'

'That wasn't very nice of him, was it? Imagine, sending a level-zero witch into such a dangerous place. They can't think very highly of you at the academy, can they?'

'I don't know,' said Molly. 'I just do as I'm told.'

'Hmm,' Belladonna thought for a moment. 'Then again, I wonder if you're telling me the whole truth, Molly Miggins. I mean, when I tried to get into your mind, I was pushed out and somehow you managed to get past the curse and the door password, all on your own. How did you manage that, Hmm?'

'I was just lucky I suppose,' said Molly.

'Lucky? Ah, I see. And the *Mind Trap*?'

'That was my grandma's doing,' said Molly. 'She's always getting into my head; I think you must have been caught up in her *Telepathy* spell.'

Belladonna nodded. 'I see, that would explain the bees.' Her face hardened for a moment, then she relaxed again and giggled. 'Between you and me, I don't like bees.'

'Nor do I… much,' said Molly.

'So, tell me about this bit of luck you had at my front door.' Belladonna clasped her hands on her lap, covering her wand. She caught Molly looking again. 'I really wouldn't bother trying to steal it. I've got at least five clones of him about the place… or is it six?'

'I guessed the password was Morgana,' said Molly. 'It wasn't hard really, she was your boss and your best friend, wasn't she?'

'IS my boss… best friend, no, I don't think so, I don't have a best friend… You could be my best friend if you wanted to be, Molly Miggins, what do you think about that?'

'Erm, that would be, erm, very nice,' said Molly.

'Good, that's settled then, we're best friends now. So, Molly Miggins, as my best friend, are you going to tell me about this other bit of luck you had when you got inside. The bit of luck that meant my curse didn't work?'

'Aunt Willow removed the curse,' said Molly. 'My Great Aunt came with me as far as the kitchen, but she wouldn't go any further, she's afraid of heights and when she opened up the cellar steps she was too scared to go down them. She went back to tell the others that I had got in.'

'My, oh my, what a bunch of cowards,' said Belladonna. 'Sending a level-zero witch to do their dirty work. It isn't fair, my dear,' she patted Molly on the knee. 'It really isn't.'

Belladonna got to her feet.

'Come with me, I want to show you something.'

She turned Molly to the right and ordered her to open the door that was now in front of her. Molly did as she was told and walked through the doorway into another brick chamber. The room was completely empty, but on the floor was a circle, drawn in chalk. Around its edges were lots of magical symbols and words that Molly couldn't decipher. Belladonna closed the door behind her and led Molly to the centre of the circle, then she stepped outside the magic symbols and pointed her wand at Molly's feet.

'Look down,' she ordered.

Molly looked at her feet and Belladonna fired a multi-coloured spell from her wand. The stone floor seems to melt away leaving Molly standing over a deep pit. She threw her arms wide as dizziness overtook her.

'Don't worry, little one. You won't fall in. You almost certainly would do in a few hours' time, but not yet.'

'What... How... Where does it lead?' asked Molly.

As Belladonna smiled, Molly noticed that her skin had lost a little bit of its firmness. It seemed looser around her eyes. Her voice had lost a little bit of its sweetness too.

'It's the way into, or out of, The Void, my dear.' Belladonna laughed a cruel laugh. 'I hoped to have finished this Void-breach in my own, normal lifetime, but sadly I reached the verge of death just hours before the aperture was ready to open. I was so angry I can tell you. Anyway I came up with the idea of holding onto a little bit of life by becoming a wraith. At the moment before my death, I cast a spell and my spirit body appeared, while my own body was still on the earth. That body-shell has long gone, turned to dust, but I survived in wraith form and started to plan for the future. I scoured my magic books looking for a spell that could help me regain my witchiness and I hit on something that would give me ninety percent of my power back, if only during the hours of darkness. It was better than nothing, don't you think? Anyway, I figured that when Morgana returned, she'd find a way to give me back my full capabilities. She's very good like that.'

She sighed, happily.

'Where was I? Oh yes, I remember. I was looking for a spell to help me, wasn't I? Well, it took centuries; I made lots of plans and scrapped them when a better one came along, then I came up with the *Mind Trap* idea. The trouble was, no one ever came near the place. Everyone was too terrified of the curse. I thought I'd shot myself in the foot by casting it to be honest.'

Belladonna put her delicate fingers to her chin and thought for a moment.

'I think that meddling wizard of yours came by one day, but he was of no use to me, he was too powerful, a threat more than an asset. Thankfully, he couldn't get inside, or I might have been discovered and my carefully laid plans, thwarted.'

Belladonna walked around the edge of the pit, her eyes never left Molly for a second.

'Then someone built a fence around my beautiful gardens and I set the *Mind Trap* on the gates. I knew it would only be a matter of time before some nosy parker came too close for their own good. I thought it was going to be you to start with, I really did, but that meddling grandmother of yours got in the way and I had to settle for Henrietta.'

Molly had been listening whilst trying her hardest not to look down into the deep, dark abyss beneath her feet. Suddenly she felt a vibration run through her boots. She held out her hands to steady herself, then leapt out of the circle.

'What was that?' she asked as a deep crash was heard from inside the pit

'Oh we're nearly there now. Just a few hours more. That noise was my spell breaking through another layer of rock. By my estimations The Void will be breached sometime in the next thirty minutes, then I can start the beacon spell and signal to Morgana and her army, so they know where I am.'

Belladonna hugged herself.

'Oh I'm so excited. I can't wait to see her. She'll reward me, I know she will. She'll give me back my life. I want to eat an apple. Do you know how long it's been since I last ate an apple?'

'Are you sure you'll be rewarded,' said Molly, desperately trying to think of something that might make Belladonna close down the spell. 'I mean; you've made her wait a few hundred years longer than she expected. She might not be too happy with you.'

'She'll understand,' snapped Belladonna. 'I thought you were my best friend, but you're not, you're just a jealous, zero-grade, junior witch who doesn't like to see me happy.'

Belladonna put a hand on Molly's shoulder and marched her back through to the other room.

'Climb inside,' she ordered, pointing at the empty cage with her wand.

Molly climbed into the dome-shaped cage. Belladonna slammed the door shut and locked it with a spell.

'I'll teach you to play fast and loose with my friendship,' she said. 'When I come back, I think I'll try your life force for size. When Morgana gets here I'll get to suck the life out of a new witch every night until she can find a way to bring me back for good, but until then, I'll just have to make do with you.'

She looked at Molly, sternly. While they had been in the pit room, bags had appeared under her eyes and her nose was longer, and more hooked, her fingers were skinnier and her voice had more of a croak to it. Molly took a quick look at Henrietta, who appeared to look much younger than she had before.

The life force spell isn't lasting the whole night, thought Molly.

Belladonna turned away and shuffled back into the pit room. Molly looked desperately towards the pile of logs that Wonky had slid under. She only had half an hour before Belladonna switched on the welcoming beacon for Morgana. She had to get her wand back somehow or the game was up.

Chapter Sixteen

When Belladonna had gone, Molly focussed her attention on the firewood pile and sent out a telepathic message to her wand.

Wonky, can you hear me?

I can hear you, Molly Miggins.

I'm going to try to move you remotely, Wonky. We have to do something about this or Morgana will be back by morning.

I'm ready when you are, Molly Miggins; try the remote command.

Molly took a look over her shoulder to make sure that Belladonna was still busy, then she turned her thoughts to her wand. She pictured him in her mind stuck, under the pile of wood and sent a thought out to try to move him. Under the woodpile the wand wiggled from side to side and slid backwards an inch.

How are we doing, Wonky?

That was good, Molly Miggins but I'm lying at an angle of about 30 degrees now and my tip is caught on a splinter of wood. Try to straighten me up a little by moving me to the left.

Molly sent out the thought and Wonky straightened up slightly.

That's it, Molly Miggins, I think I can see candlelight now so if you try to withdraw me in a straight line, that should be it.

Molly concentrated hard and sent out a thought to the wand. He began to slide along the floor towards the light. When one silver tip was visible, Belladonna walked back into the room. She stopped by the door to the pit room looking pleased with herself.

'Things are going extremely well. The way things are going, Morgana will be here an hour or so after dawn. I have a sneaky little plan that will speed things up a bit though. Shall I tell you what it is?'

Belladonna walked across the room and stood with her back to the woodpile. Her left foot came to rest no more than a centimetre away from Molly's wand.

Molly tried not to look at Belladonna's feet.

'Yes, I'd like to know what you're up to,' Molly said.

Belladonna unlocked Henrietta's cage with a quick *Unlock* spell and led the zombie-like figure to the centre of the room. Henrietta was looking a lot better, most of the wrinkles had gone, and her hair was almost blonde again.

'I'm going to use her to boost the beacon spell at the bottom of the pit,' she said. 'The spell tends to lose a bit of strength when it's surrounded by rock, so

I'll use our friend here to boost the signal out into The Void. The bonus is, we'll be able to use her eyes to project an image onto the wall of the pit room, so we can actually see Morgana's army as it approaches. Clever stuff, hey?'

'Very clever,' said Molly. 'How will you get Henrietta down the pit and back, though?'

'I'll just levitate her down there, she won't be hurt, she'd be of no use to me at all if she was. As for coming back. I'll leave that up to Morgana. She may want to keep her as a slave, to do a bit of cleaning, wax the wands, clean out cauldrons, that sort of thing. She'd be useless as a witch, so it rules that out.' Belladonna walked over to the barrels and sat down. Her knees made exactly the same noise that Granny Whitewand's knees made when she bent them.

Molly was shocked at how much Belladonna had aged in the past few minutes. Her skin hung over the bones of her face, her hands were wrinkled, her fingernails were broken. She pointed a knobbly jointed, skinny finger at Henrietta. 'I think it's time I took a little more of that life force, don't you?'

Belladonna aimed Stinger at Henrietta and croaked a spell that Molly couldn't quite make out. Pink smoke drifted from her wand and surrounded Henrietta. Belladonna raised both hands in the air and stood as if she was about to make a star jump. The change took place very quickly and a few seconds later, she lowered her arms and turned back to Molly.

'There, am I beautiful again?'

'You're younger looking if that's what you mean,' said Molly, who didn't really want to pay her a compliment after stealing Henrietta's life force.

Molly glanced at Henrietta. She had shrunk. Her hair had turned white and the flesh hung from her face. Belladonna gave her a push in the back and she obediently shuffled forwards towards the pit room.

'Back soon,' said Belladonna. 'I'll just stick our little friend at the bottom of the pit and set up the beacon boost. Don't go anywhere without me, will you?' Belladonna laughed her musical sounding laugh and followed Henrietta through the door.

Molly immediately turned her attention back towards Wonky.

Right, Wonky, I'm going to slide you out from under the wood, then try a Retrieve spell. Are you ready?

I'm ready.

Molly concentrated hard, the wand slid out until half its charred, slightly-twisted length was free of the woodpile.

Look out Molly Miggins, she's coming back.

Molly turned to the left to face Belladonna trying desperately to get her to look in her direction as she entered the room. If she looked towards the woodpile she'd see Wonky for sure.

'Don't you ever get hungry?' she asked.

Belladonna looked sad.

'Not hungry as such, but there are times when I'd do anything to be able to bite into an apple. Most of these barrels are full of them. Ripe juicy apples.' Belladonna drooled. She wiped her mouth on the back of her sleeve. 'I did hope that when I took some life force from our friend in there, that I'd be able to sink my teeth into an apple again. But I can't. I'll have to wait until Morgana restores me fully for that pleasure.' The witch gave Molly her best smile.

'I could give you an apple if you wanted one, but that would leave me one short when I do get to eat again, so I'm not going to.'

'I'm not really that hungry anyway,' said Molly, who didn't fancy eating a four-hundred-year old apple, even if it had been kept fresh by a spell.

'That's all right then,' said Belladonna, who seemed to have picked up a few of Henrietta's traits. Meanness among them.

'Don't you ever feel like going out?' asked Molly. 'You must be ready for some fresh air by now.'

'I've been able to get out into the garden, as far as the fence,' replied Belladonna, 'but I haven't dared go further than that in case I'm caught outside when the sun comes up.'

'That's a shame,' said Molly. 'You do have a lovely garden, but it must get boring being in one place all the time. You must miss flying down to the coast; it's only a minute away by broom. I had a lovely…'

Molly tailed off. If Belladonna knew she could fly she'd realise that she wasn't a level-zero witch at all.

'A lovely what?' asked Belladonna.

'A lovely… piece of fruit cake at Aunt Willow's yesterday.'

'I *LOVE* fruit cake,' said Belladonna. 'Was there any apple in it?'

'Lots,' said Molly, who didn't think there was any in it at all.

Belladonna got to her feet and began to pace the room.

'I've got a lovely broom upstairs in the kitchen. Did you see it when you came in? I made it myself. It's the fastest broom in the Black Academy… or at least it used to be, when there was a Black Academy.'

'I did see it. It's a lovely broom. I bet it goes like the wind.'

'I love my broom,' said Belladonna. 'I'd give anything to ride it again. That's the first thing I'm going to do when Morgana makes me whole.' She thought for a moment. 'The first *TWO* things I'm going to do. Fly, and eat a juicy apple.'

'I'll just go and check on progress,' said Belladonna. 'I'm expecting Morgana just before dawn now that I've set up the beacon booster.'

Molly did a quick calculation. By her reckoning it was about midnight. That meant she only had about four and a half hours to overcome Belladonna, rescue Henrietta from the pit and then seal it, forever.

She turned her attention towards Wonky again.

Are you ready, Wonky, I'll try the Retrieve spell.

Don't try just yet, Molly Miggins, I can see Belladonna from here, she's about to return. You had better push me back under the wood again.

Molly concentrated hard and slid the wand back underneath the pile of wood cuttings. The old witch reappeared just as the last bit of Wonky's silver tip slid out of sight.

Belladonna seemed agitated when she got back.

'Nothing to report. They're not in view yet,' she said. 'I reckon it'll be somewhere around four o'clock in the morning. That means we've got a bit of a wait. Shall we pass the time playing spell games... she looked down towards the woodpile where Wonky had been just a few moments before. 'Oh, sorry, you can't, can you? You don't have a wand. Silly me.'

Molly played dumb. 'Spell games, what are they?'

'You really are a novice aren't you?' said Belladonna. 'Look, forget I said anything. I'll find something else to do to pass the time.' She looked at Molly and licked her lips. 'Get some rest now; I want you nice and fresh when I draw off your life force in the morning. I want to look my best for Morgana.'

While Belladonna paced the room, Molly leaned back against the bars of the cage and pretended to sleep. It wasn't long before she heard the old witch talking to herself.

'I wonder if I can go beyond the boundaries now that I'm not in true wraith form? I don't see any reason why I shouldn't be able to... It would be so nice to be up in the sky again, to feel the wind in my hair, the salt-water spray on my face.'

Her pace grew a little faster as she walked back and forth across the room.

'I can be back well before dawn. As long as I'm here when Morgana is ready to leave The Void it will be fine. I could just nip out for an hour or two... what's to stop me?'

Molly watched out of the corner of her eye as Belladonna weighed things up.

'What about the people at the gate, though? Her grandmother is a crafty one, then there's that Aunt Willow, the one who makes cakes, I don't know much about her. That man wasn't very forthcoming when I tried to get him in the *Mind Trap*. I couldn't really get into his head at all, and that other woman only really let me see what she wanted me to see, there's a lot of witch-power in her, I reckon. Can I risk it? If they see me leave, they'll be in here like a shot.'

Belladonna suddenly stopped dead.

'*IF they see me leave…* that's it. What if they don't see me leave? What if they see young Molly Miggins leave instead? What will they do then? I think they'd want to know what she was up to, and if they have brooms they might follow, but my broom is the fastest broom that was ever made. Let them try.'

Belladonna laughed long and hard, then she turned towards Molly and held her wand above her own head. '*Doppelganger*,' she said.

Molly bit her tongue to stop an exclamation coming out of her mouth as she saw a mirror image of herself standing in front of her. The new Molly ran her wand along the bars of the cage making them rattle. Molly sat up and yawned.

'What time is it?' she asked.

'Time for a nice long broomstick ride,' said the Belladonna-Molly. 'I've waited three, witch-lifetimes for this.' She left the room, humming to herself.

Chapter Seventeen

The second that Belladonna left the room, Molly got to her knees and remotely addressed her wand.

We need to hurry, Wonky, I have to telepath Aunt Willow or Granny Whitewand to let them know I'm okay and it's not me leaving the house.

Ready when you are, Molly Miggins.

Molly concentrated hard and Wonky gently slid out from beneath the pile of sawn-up timber. She held her hand out of the bars of the cage and called *Retrieve*, in her mind. Wonky suddenly shot up into the air, flew across the room, and hit the palm of Molly's hand with a Thwack! She gripped the wand tight and immediately fired an unlock spell on the cage.

The door remained shut.

'Bother,' said Molly.

'She used a combination lock spell,' said Wonky. 'Give me a minute and I'll work it out.'

'Can we do the *Telepathy* spell first, Wonky?' asked Molly.

'Certainly,' said the wand. 'I can work out the unlock-code at the same time.'

Molly concentrated hard and called the *Advanced Telepath* spell. 'Calling Granny Whitewand, calling Granny Whitewand, come in, Granny Whitewand.'

Molly found herself inside a shadowy room. It was oblong in shape and had a carpet with one curled-up corner on the floor. On it, sat a box full of old papers and scrolls. Curtains billowed in from two open windows. At the far end of the room was a fireplace with a comfy-looking armchair in front. The top of a witch's hat was visible over the back of the chair. A loud, wheezy snoring told Molly just who was sitting in it.

'Granny Whitewand, I need you to pass a message to Mum, Dad and Aunt Willow.'

The snoring stopped abruptly.

'What are you doing here, Millie?' Are you telepathing whilst flying? That's very dangerous. If the witch wardens see you, you'll lose your licence.'

'It wasn't me leaving the house, Grandma,' said Molly urgently. 'That's what I wanted to tell you.'

'Of course it was you, we saw you take off, it was definitely you.' Granny Whitewand got out of the chair and turned to face Molly.

'It was Belladonna,' said Molly. 'She used a *Doppelganger* spell. I'm stuck in a cage inside the cottage. Belladonna is running the spell to open The Void, she's using Henrietta to attract Morgana's army.'

'Right,' said Granny Whitewand, 'that's it, we're coming in. We'll ambush her when she gets back.'

'No, that's no good,' said Molly. 'The place is too small and with all that magic in such a confined space, someone is bound to get hurt. I don't want it to be one of us.'

'What do you want us to do then?' asked Granny Whitewand. 'We can't just leave you there, locked in a cage.'

'I'll be out soon, Grandma. Wonky's working on the combination spell so you'll see me in a short while. The thing is, Morgana is due to reach The Void breach just before dawn, so I need Belladonna in the cottage to remove the spell she's put on Henrietta, a good while before then. I might be able to remove it myself of course; I'm going to try in a few moments. The problem is, we don't know which spell she used on her, so it might be difficult. If I can get Henrietta out of the pit, I'll try to seal The Void opening. If I can't, then we'll have to play it by ear. I more or less talked Belladonna into going for a broomstick ride. I had to get her out of the way so that I could talk to you and let you know I'm all right. I couldn't do that while she was in the house.'

Molly grinned as Wonky winked at her to let her know he'd cracked the combination code.

'Grandma, I've got a bit of a plan, if I need to use it, but it still needs a lot of work. I'll give it some more thought, then let you know what I've come up with.'

'Is there anything we can do to help you, Millie,' asked Granny Whitewand.

'Only one thing, Grandma,' said Molly.

'What's that?' asked Granny Whitewand.

'Stop calling me Millie.'

Molly shut down the *Telepathy* spell and spoke to her wand.

'Well, Wonky, what's the code?' she asked.

'111,' replied Wonky. 'I got it almost immediately. Her passwords aren't up to much, are they?'

Molly pointed Wonky at the cage door and called *Unlock 111*. The door swung open and she climbed out. She ran through to the pit room and stared down into the depths.

'Can you work out how to reverse the spell that put Henrietta down there, Wonky?' she asked.

Wonky concentrated hard for a full minute.

'No, I can't work it out, Molly Miggins. She used a combination of *Beacon*, which I can pick up, with something else, which I can't. I'm sorry. I also think she may have booby-trapped the spell, so that if anyone tries to remove it and uses the wrong words, something awful will happen.'

'We can't risk it then, Wonky,' said Molly. She looked at the wall in front, where a video image was being projected via Henrietta's eyes from the bottom of the pit.

'Still no sign of Morgana, that's good news. We have some time left.'

'Indeed we do, Molly Miggins,' replied the wand. 'There's hope yet.'

'There is one thing I'd like to know, Wonky. How will I go about sealing The Void when the time comes? I've always used a new spell to do it in the past.'

'Just pick one of the previous spells, Molly Miggins, they're all super-powerful *Seal* spells. Any of them should work here.'

Molly breathed a sigh of relief. 'That's some good news at least, Wonky. Right, let's go and see if we can find Belladonna. I've got a crafty plan, hatching in the back of my mind, but before I can put it into practice, I need to know where she is.'

Molly called for a bright *Glow in the Dark* spell and raced through the storeroom. She took off her hat and ducked as she made her way along the narrow passage, and she took her time climbing the steep staircase. The flagstone was closed when she arrived near the top, but she spotted a lever on the wall and when she pulled it, the flagstone slid back.

Molly climbed out into the kitchen and ran for the front door. She spotted her family at the gates as she hurtled out into the garden. She waved to them, then ran around the side of the house and picked up her broom. She quickly straddled it and hit the twigs, three times.

'*Fly, Fly, Fly,*' she cried.

The broom rose into the air and shot forward. Molly steered it to the gates and hovered above her family for a few moments.

'I have to get Belladonna back inside the cottage well before dawn or Morgana's hordes will be out on the lawn,' she shouted. 'I couldn't seal The Void because Henrietta is still in there and I don't know which spell Belladonna used. I'm going to have to find her and trick her into releasing Henrietta, if I can.'

'How can we help, Molly?' asked Aunt Willow. 'Do you want us to try to release that silly girl?'

'No,' said Molly. 'We think Belladonna has put a booby-trap on the spell, so only she can lift it. I have got a plan though, and I'll need you all to help me make it work. I'll going to require some of your stage-illusion magic, Dad,' she added. 'We'll need some mirrors, as many as you can find.'

'Mirrors?' Mr Miggins looked confused.

'It's for an illusion, Dad, get me as many as you can, big ones, small ones, any size or shape. We're going to need at least a dozen, more if you can find them.'

'I've got my stage props in the car, Molly,' said Mr Miggins, 'there are a few big ones in there, and there are at least ten mirrors at Aunt Willow's house. I'll get them down here.'

'Mum, I think it's time to smash those padlocks and get those gates open,' said Molly. 'Belladonna's *Mind Trap* night not work when she's concentrating on flying.'

'What about the *Protect* spell, Molly, that's still running isn't it?' said Mrs Miggins.

'Bother,' said Molly. 'I'll have to remove it when I get back. I'd forgotten about that. It has to be removed or she won't fall for the illusion I have planned.'

'Do you want me to remove it, Molly?' said Mrs Miggins.

'No, I'll do it,' replied Molly. 'I actually want her to see me lift the spell. The illusion will work so much better if she thinks daylight can get into the house.'

She steadied her broom. 'Hide the mirrors near the house; make sure Belladonna can't see them when she gets back. Meet me at the Woodhenge circle in an hour but don't stay out in the open, hide in that little wood at the side. I'm going to find Belladonna and try to lure her over there. See you later.'

Molly rose high into the sky, and without looking back, set course for the coast.

Chapter Eighteen

Molly flew across the fields, past the small wood and the Woodhenge circle, then swept along the cliff edge. There was no sign of Belladonna.

'Bother,' she said aloud. 'I thought she'd be flying along the coast, Wonky, she said she liked the sea air.'

'It's a long coast, Molly Miggins,' replied the wand. 'She'll be here somewhere. I guarantee it.'

The bright, full moon that had lit up the landscape suddenly disappeared behind a thick, dark cloud and the light dimmed noticeably. Out to sea, storm clouds were gathering and the wind was picking up. Molly hit several pockets of turbulence as she flew along the outreaches of the bay. She let the broom drift downwards and flew out to sea riding on the spray, just above the waves. When she reached the far shore, she took the broom up to cliff level before circling the whole bay again.

By the time she reached the cliffs near Woodhenge, the heavy rain-clouds had rolled in and the moon had vanished. Molly couldn't make out anything further than a few yards ahead. She fired up a *Torchlight* spell and a strong beam of light lit up the area in front. She waved the wand left and right as she flew but there was no sign of Belladonna.

She was just about to turn around and fly back to the bay when she heard the whoosh of a broom coming alongside and the mad cackle of a witch. A *Fireball* crashed into the back of her broom sending her into a tailspin. She fought against the spin with all her might but she was falling at high speed and the ground seemed to be rising up to meet her. Molly hit the broom hard with her wand and straightened out just a couple of feet above the rocks at the edge of the cliff face. She tucked her knees under her chin and placed both feet on the broom shaft as she hurtled through the long grass. Molly looked over her shoulder as a *Thunderbolt* sped towards her. She veered to the right, then managed to get a bit of lift. The Thunderbolt crashed into the grass leaving a large, smouldering patch of brown earth.

Molly veered left, then swerved right as another *Fireball* left Belladonna's wand. She issued a *Harrier* command and the broom came to a dead halt, then, less than a second later, it shot straight up, one hundred feet into the air. Belladonna sat on her broom, mouth agape. Molly took advantage of her confusion and fired off a *Meteor spell* of her own. The spell smashed into Belladonna's midriff, the broom dropped forty feet before she managed to gain control again. By this time, Molly was in the air directly above her. She fired another *Fireball* but the old witch steered left and the spell whistled past her hat, Belladonna used a sneaky *Illusion* spell and suddenly there were three different Belladonnas to aim at. Molly chose the centre one and shot off a Thunderbolt which whistled straight through the target. She fired again at the left-side Belladonna, with the same result. Molly realised she was heading for the tall trees at the edge of the wood and had to change course to avoid it. By the time she swung back around to face the open sea again, Belladonna was above her, and in a position of strength.

Molly thought fast and conjured up her very first *Polar Storm* spell. Suddenly the warm, soft eddy currents around the cliff top were transformed into a raging storm. Blinding snow swept across the landscape. Molly held on to her broom tightly and dropped to grass level where the air was a little more stable. She skimmed across the grasslands and came out of the storm into the calm of the bay. She could see Belladonna's broom being tossed around in the eye of the storm. Then it fell out of the sky.

Molly waited until the winds had dropped and the spell had burned itself out before flying gently down to the ground. She landed at the edge of the old henge, laid down her broom and walked to the centre of the circle, where Belladonna lay in a crumpled heap on the floor.

Molly approached, warily. Belladonna was lying with her right arm under her body, her broom was about five feet away.

'Are you all right?' asked Molly.

Belladonna just moaned.

Molly took a couple of steps closer and put her hand on the old witch's shoulder.

'Are you all rig–'

Belladonna leapt upright with surprising agility. She grabbed Molly by the clasp of her cloak, whipped her wand arm up, and pointed Stinger into Molly's face.

'Drop the wand,' she ordered.

Molly did as she was told. Behind her she could hear the sound of legs brushing through long grass.

'Right, Molly Miggins, or whatever your real name is. I think it's time we had a proper, honest chat, don't you?'

Molly nodded.

Belladonna pushed her so that she stepped backwards, away from Wonky. She lowered her wand and pointed it to Molly's chest. 'So, you're a zero-level witch are you? Flying as well as that. Firing off missiles like that. Casting snow storm spells like that. I don't believe it. You've been telling me lies, haven't you?'

'I never said I was a zero-level witch,' said Molly, 'you said that. I just went along with it.'

'You made out you were my best friend, but you never were.'

'Again, it was you that made that suggestion,' said Molly. She contacted Wonky, remotely.

Get ready, Wonky.

Ready when you are, Molly Miggins.

'You told me that Henrietta was your senior,' whined Belladonna. 'I thought she had more power than you, that's why I used her in the pit,' she looked at Molly angrily. 'I should have put you there.'

'We all make mistakes,' said Molly with a smile.

Come to me, Molly sent a telepathic command to her wand. *Retrieve.*

Before Belladonna could blink, Wonky was back in Molly's hand. She caught the wand, lifted her arm and aimed it at Belladonna's face, all in one movement.

'We appear to be in a bit of a standoff,' said Molly.

'That was very impressive,' admitted Belladonna. 'Actually, I don't know where we go from here. One of us will lose, that's for sure.'

Molly had a close look at Belladonna. Her face was beginning to fade again. Her cheeks looked sallow, bags were forming under her eyes, her chin had become elongated and her nose had a definite hook. Her green wart was back, a handful of short wiry hairs sprouted from it.

'It looks like you need a top-up,' said Molly. 'Sadly, for you, there's no one around for you to steal any life force from.'

'There's you,' cackled Belladonna. 'Don't think you've won yet; you haven't.'

'Are you all right, Molly?' called a voice from the gloom.

'I'm fine, Granny Whitewand. I'm in the circle with Belladonna. We could use a little light here, it's pitch black.'

As a faint glow appeared over the circle, Molly took a quick look out of the corner of her eye. Mr and Mrs Miggins, Great Aunt Willow and Granny Whitewand stood in a group on the outside of the henge. Granny Whitewand was holding her wand aloft, a grey spell poured out from it.

'Could you all spread out, around the circle, please,' asked Molly. 'But keep your wands aimed at her.'

High Witch Miggins, Great Aunt Willow and Professor Miggins, spread out at equal distances around the ancient circle. When they were in place, Molly took a step back, closed her eyes, and concentrated.

The air around them began to move and a thin mist developed. Shapes moved around inside it. Molly could once again hear the chanting of the ancient druids.

'Lady of the light, we see you,' said a voice.

'Darkness visits the circle,' said Molly, 'it brings bad magic.'

The druid lifted his staff and waved it slowly in front of him.

'The darkness has no power in the circle while the lady of the light is within,' said the druid. 'Gwitha war kelgh'

'Thank you,' said Molly.

The mist lifted and Molly was once again alone with Belladonna.

'Give me the wand, please, Belladonna.' Molly held out her hand.

'Give you my… I'll tell you what I'll give you…' Belladonna almost screamed out the *Thunderbolt* command.

Nothing happened.

Belladonna looked down the end of her wand as if a bullet had got stuck there. She aimed and tried again with the same result.

'You have no power while you are in this circle,' said Molly.

'Nonsense,' spat Belladonna. She smacked the wand against her thigh and tried another spell.

Nothing came out of the wand.

'Keep your wands on her just in case,' called Molly. 'I just want a quick word with Grandma.'

Molly turned away and walked to the edge of the circle where her grandmother was still casting the light spell. Belladonna saw her chance and tried to run. Two *Fireballs* smashed into the ground at her feet.

'I wouldn't try that again,' said Great Aunt Willow. 'I was crowned best marksman at the Deppbury Witch-Fair, five years running. I can knock the tail off a mouse at a hundred paces.'

Belladonna squatted down on her haunches and sulked. She looked at her bony, wrinkled hands with their twisted, broken nails and shouted in anger. 'My beautiful hands, look what you've done to them.'

'They were Henrietta's more than yours,' said Mrs Miggins.

'She wanted to share, honestly,' said Belladonna. 'Ask her.'

Molly shook her head in disbelief as she heard Belladonna's wild claims.

'What can I do for you, Millie,' asked granny Whitewand.

'Molly, Grandma, it's M O L L Y,' Molly spelled her name out slowly.

'This is no time to be picky,' said Granny Whitewand.

Molly sighed, then smiled. She gave her grandmother a big hug.

'Whatever would I do without you?' she said.

Granny Whitewand wiped a tear from her cheek. 'Enough of the mushiness, we've got a dangerous witch to deal with.'

'She's no danger while she's in the circle,' said Molly. 'The ancient folk are seeing to that. She's losing power all the time as she ages, too, Grandma.' She leaned close to her grandmother's ear and whispered. 'When I give the signal could you rustle up the Dawn Chorus?'

'The Dawn Chorus?' whispered Granny Whitewand, 'why do you want a lot of birds singing?'

'I want to make her think that it's later than it actually is,' said Molly. 'Start with a single bird, then another, and another, gently at first, so we can hardly hear it. Try to make it sound like it's coming from the wood over there, if you can.'

'Will do, Millie. What's the signal going to be?'

'I'll take off my hat.' Molly smiled and walked around to Mr Miggins.

'Dad,' she whispered. 'Did you get the mirrors?'

'I've got about twenty of them, Molly. We slid them through the gates then we flew over and carried them up to the cottage. They're hidden behind the Hawthorn bush near the front door.'

'Thanks, Dad,' said Molly. 'When we go back, and after I remove the *Protect* spell, can you set them up at the angles needed to send a beam of light right into Belladonna's pit room?'

'I haven't been inside yet, Molly, but as you know from watching my stage act. I can use mirrors to bend light, or images, anywhere.'

'Perfect,' said Molly. 'I'll leave it to you, Mum and Great Aunt Willow to set up, while I and Granny Whitewand force her to release Henrietta.'

Mr Miggins scratched his head. 'What do you want the light for, Molly? I don't quite understand.'

'For insurance,' said Molly. 'Just in case she decides not to help us.'

She gave her father a big hug. 'Keep your eyes on Belladonna, we're going to show her a Molly Miggins style illusion,' she whispered.

Next, Molly walked around to Great Aunt Willow. She gave her a big hug.

'Thanks for helping me out, Aunt Willow,' she began. 'Could you do me a favour; I need you and Mum to set something up for me.'

'Anything, Molly, just ask,' she said.

'When you hear Granny Whitewand's bird song, can you cast a *Warm Glow* spell for me. You've got your back to the east, and that's where the sun rises. It would be great if you could make it cover a nice wide area and give it a shiny, golden core, so it looks just like the start of the sunrise.'

'I can do that, Molly,' said Aunt Willow. 'What's the signal?'

'I'll take my hat off,' said Molly.

She walked a little further around the circle and gave her mother a big hug.

'Mum, Granny Whitewand and Aunt Willow are going to help me set up an illusion in a few moments. Could you help out and create a soft breeze and maybe some dew on the grass inside the circle?'

Mrs Miggins nodded eagerly. 'Of course I can, Molly. Will you give me a signal?'

'I'll take off my hat,' said Molly.

'What are you hoping to achieve with this illusion, Molly?' Mrs Miggins looked at her daughter proudly.

'I'm going to make her think that the sun's coming up an hour early,' said Molly.

Chapter Nineteen

Molly walked back to the centre of the circle with the air of someone who knew they were in complete control of things. Belladonna was surly when Molly approached.

'I don't know how you think any of this is going to help you. Morgana will be here soon, then you'll know about it. She'll snap your cheap old wand in front of your eyes. I'll probably be given the decision about what happens to you, so I'd think very carefully about that before you do anything else.'

Molly squatted down so that she was eye-to-eye with what had now become a very old hag.

'Oh, I don't think you will have to think too hard about what to do with me. For one thing, Morgana and I are old friends. We've met quite a few times over the past year. For another thing, this ancient lump of wood is actually Cedron, the most famous wand that ever existed. The wand that won the Witch Wars. The wand that sent Morgana and the entire Black Academy to the centre of The Void. So I'd think very carefully about what *YOU* do next if I was you.'

Belladonna's rheumy old eyes opened wide.

'Cedron? I don't believe a word of it. Why would they give such a famous wand to the likes of you?'

'They didn't mean to, I'll admit that,' said Molly. 'But we are a team now; no one can ever take him away from me. So, as I said, I would be very careful about what you say, and what you do.'

Belladonna eyed Wonky curiously. 'So, even if that's true, you can't claim to have met Morgana.'

Molly crossed her fingers and held them up in front of Belladonna's face. 'We're like that, me and Morgana,' she said. 'You last saw her, let me see… about four hundred years ago? Am I right?'

Belladonna nodded.

'Well I saw her just last month,' said Molly. She was just about to come out of a breach in The Void, in a land far away from here.'

Belladonna frowned. 'She was about to come out? So why is she still seeking the exit that I've made for her?'

'That will be because I sealed the breach to stop her getting out,' said Molly. 'It's the second time I've done that. She wasn't very happy with me on either occasion.'

'You… a young… slip of a thing, hardly out of your nappies, thwarted the Great Morgana? I don't think so,' Belladonna shook her head. 'No, I don't think so.'

'You might get the chance to ask her about it one day,' said Molly as though she didn't care whether she got the chance or not. 'One thing's for certain, it will never happen at all if you don't hand over your wand and surrender to me this minute.'

'What good is my wand?' asked Belladonna, sulkily. 'It doesn't work.'

'It doesn't work in this circle,' said Molly, 'and by the way you're ageing, I'm not so sure how well it will work outside of it. You're very nearly a true wraith again, Belladonna, and you know what that means.' Molly looked up at the sky. 'If you're still here when the sun comes up… well… I wouldn't want to be you, let's put it that way.'

'Ha! You don't scare me,' said Belladonna. 'Morgana and her army will be here before dawn. You and your pathetic family will be running for your lives.'

'Really?' Molly looked around. 'She's a bit on the late side, isn't she?'

'She'll be here before dawn,' spat Belladonna. 'It's at least an hour and a half away.'

Molly cocked her head to the side, as though she was listening for something.

'I think you might have lost track of the time while you were sea-surfing,' she said. 'Dawn is actually, about a minute or so away. I thought I heard the first blackbird stirring then. Didn't you?'

'You can't fool me like that,' said Belladonna, 'I've got a built-in clock, and it's never wrong.'

Molly took off her hat and scratched her head. Granny Whitewand, Aunt Willow and Mrs Miggins, cast their secret spells.

'You're telling lies,' said Belladonna. 'If I hear a bird sing, I'll eat my hat.'

The faint sound of a blackbird filtered across the field. A gentle breeze blew across the grass depositing dew on the tips of the grass stalks. From over Great Aunt Willow's shoulder, a faint red glow appeared.

'Would you like some jam to put on it?' asked Molly.

'On what?' said Belladonna.

'Your hat,' said Molly. The birdsong got louder as different varieties of birds joined in.

Belladonna got to her feet.

'It can't be… no, I don't believe it.' She looked around in a panic. The red-glow from behind Aunt Willow became ever so slightly brighter, the gentle breeze blew the grass against her skirt, brushing droplets of water on it.

'Don't leave me out here,' she begged. 'I'll die.'

'You're already dead, but I do see the problem you have,' said Molly sympathetically. She looked over the fields towards Cranberry Cottage. 'I think I can get you back there before the sun comes up,' she said.

'We'll never make it,' wailed Belladonna. 'I'm doomed.'

'We'll make it,' said Molly, 'but first, surrender your wand, then walk to the edge of the circle and wait for me.'

Belladonna meekly handed over her wand and hobbled, painfully to the perimeter of the circle. 'Hurry,' she croaked as she stumbled along. 'The sun's almost here.'

Molly raised her hands and waved so that all her family members looked at her. 'Go back to Cranberry Cottage, quickly,' she shouted. 'I'm going to remove the *Protect* spell as soon as I get there and I'll need everything in place, soon after.'

'Our brooms are on the edge of the wood, Molly,' replied Great Aunt Willow. 'Off you go; we'll only be a couple of minutes behind you.'

'Granny Whitewand can use Belladonna's broom,' said Molly, 'I'll need Grandma with me in case she tries anything.'

'I'm on it, Millie,' cackled Granny Whitewand, who could move with surprising agility when she needed to. She hurried into the circle, straddled Belladonna's broom and took off immediately.

'Come on, slowcoach,' she called as Molly picked up her own broom.

Molly rushed to Belladonna's side and ordered her onto the broom. She tried to get on at the back, but Molly insisted she ride in front. 'I want you where I can see you,' she said.

Molly hit the broom hard and they took off sluggishly. Aunt Willow sent another *Warm Glow* spell across the circle. Belladonna screamed and pulled her cloak over her head.

'Hurry,' she wailed.

Molly aimed the broom towards the cottage, waited until Granny Whitewand came alongside, then she held Wonky in the air and made a wide circling motion. '*Zoom*,' she cried.

In an instant, both brooms covered half the distance to the cottage. Molly raised her wand and called the *Zoom* spell again, and exactly one half second later, they arrived at Cranberry Cottage.

Molly landed quickly and ushered a clearly terrified Belladonna inside. Granny Whitewand landed straight after, and hobbled towards the cottage.

'Keep an eye on her while I remove the *Protect* spell, please, Grandma,' said Molly.

Granny Whitewand grabbed Belladonna by the scruff of the neck and dragged her into the hall.

'Don't leave me here, take me down to the cellar, I'm begging you,' cried Belladonna.

'Why should I?' asked Granny Whitewand. 'Give me one good reason why I should do you a favour?'

'Because if you don't, I'll die as soon as the spell is lifted,' she wailed.

'I don't think so,' said Granny Whitewand. 'We've got a couple of minutes yet. Molly's *Zoom* spell meant we outran the sun.'

She kept hold of the shaking Belladonna's cloak, while Molly raised her wand in the doorway of the cottage.

'*Undo Protection*,' she called.

A greyish-blue smoke appeared from her wand and drifted around the room. Belladonna threw herself onto the floor and tried to crawl under her cloak. 'Nooo,' she wailed. 'Nooooo.'

The entire house groaned as though it was at last being allowed to settle on its foundations. The timbers creaked, bits of plaster fell from the walls and a huge crack appeared in the ceiling of the hall.

'We'd better get a move on before the whole place comes down,' said Molly as she heard the sound of broomsticks landing in the garden outside. Mrs Miggins appeared at the door as Molly was about to step into the kitchen.

'The grass is two feet high out there already, Molly, the property is beginning to age incredibly quickly.'

'Can you slow the process down a bit, Mum,' hissed Molly, so that Belladonna couldn't hear. 'I don't want her to know she's the owner of a crumbling ruin.'

'I'll see what I can do, Molly, I'll try a brief *Suspend Ageing* spell, but it won't last all that long.'

'Thanks, Mum, even a few extra minutes might be enough,' said Molly. She pointed to the door at the end of the passage as Mr Miggins appeared with the first batch of mirrors. Start here by the front door, Dad, the cellar steps are in the corner of the kitchen. Aunt Willow, when the mirrors are in place could you get ready to set off a remote *Bright Light* spell? I want it to look exactly like the rays of the sun if you can manage that.'

Great Aunt Willow put the pile of mirrors she was carrying, down onto the floor. 'Of course I can, Molly, but why a remote spell, why don't I just stay up here and cast it onto the first mirror?'

'Because Belladonna has to see that we are all down there, or she might smell a rat,' replied Molly. 'She'll only believe it if we're all down there with her.' Molly paused, then went on. 'There's a slight chance we won't need to use it, but I've got a feeling that Belladonna will have to be coerced into helping us. She won't do it voluntarily.'

Molly ran across the kitchen and took charge of Belladonna. It seemed to take an age to get the two old witches down the steep steps to the cellar. Molly began to wish she'd asked Aunt Willow to accompany her instead of her grandmother.

'Eventually, they reached Belladonna's storeroom.

'What's that dreadful pong?' asked Granny Whitewand. She held her nose. 'Peeew. Something's gone off.'

'My apples, my beautiful apples, they've all gone bad,' wailed Belladonna. She looked at Molly with hate-filled eyes. 'I'll get you for this, Molly Miggins,' she hissed.

Molly immediately thought of Henrietta, who had used those exact words on numerous occasions.

'I'm not so sure about that,' she replied. 'No one else has managed it yet.'

Molly gave Belladonna a push and followed her into the pit room. The old witch's eyes went immediately to the video image on the wall. She couldn't contain her excitement.

'She's nearly here. Morgana!' she yelled into the pit. 'Morgana, It's me, Belladonna, I've freed you.'

Molly's head snapped around and she watched the moving images on the wall. There was no doubt about it. She could see Morgana clearly, marching at the head of a long procession of witches.

'Any minute now,' Belladonna cackled.

'Get Henrietta out of there,' ordered Molly.

'Shan't,' said Belladonna, 'and you can't make me.'

'We'll see about that,' said Molly. She looked over her shoulder nervously. Mr Miggins appeared in the next room, closely followed by Mrs Miggins and Aunt Willow. Mr Miggins stuck up his thumb. They were ready.

Chapter Twenty

Molly pointed her wand at Belladonna. She wasn't impressed.

'It's no good waving that woodworm-ridden, lump of rotten timber in front of me,' she said. 'I'm just going to stand here and wait for Morgana to sort you out. She looked at the video playing on the wall. 'Ooh, I can hear their marching feet now, can't you?'

Molly sneaked a quick glance. Morgana was definitely closer, she pricked up her ears and listened. She was sure she heard the faint call of, 'Belladonna.'

'You'll do as I say, or you won't be here to welcome Morgana,' said Molly sternly. She pulled Belladonna's wand out of her secret pocket and held it out. 'Get Henrietta out of there, now,' she ordered.

'No,' said Belladonna. 'There's nothing you can say or do to make me, either.'

Molly turned away from her, winked at Aunt Willow and closed the pit-room door until there was only a foot-wide gap. Aunt Willow muttered a few words and the back wall of the cage-room was filled with blinding light. Molly opened the door a little wider and nodded an almost imperceptible nod to Mr Miggins. He adjusted the large square mirror on a stand at his side until the light shone onto the back of the pit chamber door.

'Maybe this will convince you,' said Molly. She eased the door open another twelve inches. A beam of brilliant-white light hit the far wall.

'W, w, what…. How?'

'It's all done with mirrors,' said Molly. 'You see, now that your *Protect* spell has been lifted, sunlight can get into your hall. We put a mirror in the hall, and another mirror near the kitchen door, which we angled, so that it reflected onto another mirror that we put by the cellar steps, that reflected down to a mirror at the bottom of the stairwell, which reflected along the passage to–'

'Stop it,' screamed Belladonna. 'I get the idea.'

Molly opened the door a little wider. The beam of light moved around the wall towards Belladonna.

'No, no, this isn't fair. Morgana is nearly here, I can't just disappear after all this time, after all this planning, not now, please… I'm so close to becoming whole once more.'

Molly offered her the wand again. Belladonna hung her head and reached out for it. Granny Whitewand aimed her own wand at Belladonna and glanced towards the beam of light. 'No tricks now, or you're cooked,' she said.

Belladonna raised her wand and muttered a few words. Molly looked over the edge of the pit and saw Henrietta rising up towards her. She cast a quick glance at the video wall but the only thing she could see was the side of the pit as Henrietta sailed past. Suddenly a voice echoed out of the hole.

'Belladonna, where is my beacon guide?'

'I'm sorry,' Belladonna squealed in a high-pitched voice. She eyed the beam of light on the back wall, nervously and took a step back.

Henrietta's floating body rose slowly out of the pit. When her feet were clear, she hovered, waiting, her eyes staring blankly ahead. She looked the same as she always had. Belladonna, in comparison, looked haggard.

Granny Whitewand shoved her wand into her secret pocket and pulled the girl away from the pit. Henrietta stood, unblinking, as Molly stepped aside and her grandmother led the zombie-like girl out of the room.

The moment they were clear of the doorway, Belladonna raised her wand and fired off a *Shut-Lock* spell. The door slammed and locked with a loud rattle. Before Molly could lift her own wand, Belladonna hit her with a *Benumb* spell. The old witch danced about with glee and screamed into the pit. 'Morgana, it's your humble servant, Belladonna. Everything is ready for your return. Welcome home.'

Chapter Twenty-One

Belladonna was a fast spell caster, but Molly was faster. The moment the *Shut-Lock* spell was invoked, she silently cast a *Protect* spell, and because it activated at exactly the same time as *Benumb* hit her body, Belladonna's spell only half worked. Molly found herself still in complete control of her mind.

Which spell has she hit me with, Wonky? I don't think I know it.

It's the Benumb, spell, Molly Miggins, an old version of Freeze. It's nothing to worry about. Cast Unfreeze and the effects will wear off very quickly.

Molly silently cast *Unfreeze* and immediately got the feeling back in her toes. The pins and needles rose up her legs, past her knees and into her hip joints. Molly waited patiently. Outwardly she appeared to be frozen to the spot with her wand arm raised above her head. She could hear the muffled voices of her parents as they cast spells at the pit-room door, trying to force it open.

Belladonna danced around the pit, occasionally shouting to Morgana, boasting about her achievements, pleading with the Black Witch to hurry; imploring her to restore her to true, witch-form.

'I have a gift for you, Morgana. A gift I know you will enjoy playing with.'

'A gift to play with?' Morgana's cruel voice wafted up from the pit. 'Do you offer me a toy?'

'Not a toy, Your Amazingness. My gift to you is a young witch. A pain-in-the-neck-witch that you may have heard of. Her name is Molly Miggins.'

'MOLLY MIGGINS!' Morgana's voice was like ice. It echoed around the pit-room. 'You have Molly Miggins?'

Belladonna cackled. 'Indeed I do, Your High and Mightiness. She is here, awaiting your pleasure.'

'Do not let her escape,' hissed Morgana. 'I have plans for this Molly Miggins, I will take my time with her, her demise will not be pleasant.'

'Don't worry, Your Stupendousness. She's not going anywhere.' Belladonna poked at Molly with a bony finger.

Molly remained staring ahead. The pins and needles had now reached her fingertips; they moved through her hand and up her wrist.

It won't be long now, Wonky, are you ready?

Ready and willing, Molly Miggins replied the wand.

Belladonna got onto her hands and knees and stuck her head into the pit.

'I am your servant, Your Marvellous Majesty. I bow down before your unimaginable power.'

Morgana's voice became even icier.

'You have served me well, Belladonna. I was extremely annoyed that it took you so many centuries to open a portal, but all that is forgotten. I am about to return at last. If the Miggins girl is at my mercy, you will be well rewarded.'

Belladonna got to her feet and did a little dance in front of Molly.

'Did you hear that? I will be rewarded. I'll be whole again. It's been so long… I'll be able to feel, to touch, to eat…' Her face became angry. 'You spoiled my apples,' she spat. 'I think I'll ask Morgana if I can watch as she takes her revenge on you. She might even let me join in.' She clicked her fingers in front of Molly's face. 'You thought you'd won, you thought you were being sooooo, clever. Well, listen to me, Molly Miggins, You're not half as clever as you think you are. You'll soon wish you had never heard the name of Belladonna Blackheart, or Cranberry Cottage.'

As she spoke a large lump of plaster fell from the ceiling. Belladonna looked up to see a huge crack appear above her head. She turned back to the pit.

'Hurry, Majesty.'

The pins and needles reached Molly's shoulder and moved to her neck.

Prepare a small Fireball, Wonky.

Fireball prepared, Molly Miggins. I'm awaiting your command.

The pins and needles cleared Molly's chin and made their way across her cheeks. She fought the urge to blink as they reached her eyelids.

A huge lump of rock fell from the wall and rolled towards the pit. Belladonna threw herself at it to prevent it falling in. She got to her feet as a long, jagged fissure almost split the wall in two.

Belladonna rushed back to the deep shaft as the image of Morgana appeared across top of the pit. Her face was ash-white, her eyes cruel and narrow, her lips were peeled back into an evil grin. The vision bubbled around the edges, like a pot of water coming to the boil. Ripples rolled across the surface.

'I AM RETURNED!' she cried.

Belladonna stood, transfixed, on the edge of the pit, her wand arm stretched out in front of her.

The pins and needles finally cleared the back of Molly's head. She blinked once, brought her wand down and let loose the *Fireball* in one movement. The red-hot spell shot out of Wonky and smashed into Belladonna's hand. Her wand fell, hit the floor and rolled into the pit.

'What? ... You ... How?'

Molly smiled a thin smile. 'It's time to end this,' she said.

Belladonna became frantic. 'No, noooooo, please. I beg you, don't spoil it now... I want to be whole again... What will I say to Morgana? She'll–'

'She'll be rather angry, I would imagine,' said Molly.

'She's here,' screamed Belladonna. 'You can't stop her now.'

'Watch me,' said Molly. She paused for a moment, then continued. 'Do you know; I think it's only fair that you should be the one to explain things to her. You must be really looking forward to seeing her after all this time.'

'No, Nooooo. Don't send me down there. She'll be too angry, she'll... Oh, I don't know what she'll do to me.'

'To be honest, I don't really care,' said Molly. She fired a *Fireball* at Belladonna's feet. The old witch hopped on one foot to avoid it, but as soon as she raised her leg, Molly fired another one. It caught Belladonna on her standing ankle; she swayed, tried to right herself, swayed again, and fell into the pit.

'NOOOOooooooooo,'

Molly turned her wand quickly towards the bubbling vision on the surface of the pit. She closed her eyes and concentrated, then spoke the words of the *Seal* spell she had used the last time she and Morgana met.

'*Dún an doras.*'

Morgana's frothing image froze for a moment, then the misty air on the surface of the pit began to swirl. Molly stood back as a local, howling, spiralling, tornado-like-wind whistled around the pit shaft, dragging in dust and rock, it spiralled faster and faster until it was nothing more than a blur. Morgana's failing voice drifted out from the whirlwind that engulfed the pit and whipped around the room. 'Molly Miggins,' it hissed. 'I will have my revenge for this.'

'Possibly,' muttered Molly to herself. 'But not today.'

The wind continued to spin; it drew down plaster and rock from the ceiling above. Molly took another rearward step and backed into the door. She could hear the frantic voices of her family on the other side who were still trying to break the *Shut Lock* spell.

'Try *Unlock 111*,' Molly sent a telepathic message to Granny Whitewand.

'Will do, Millie,' replied her very flustered grandmother.

The door flew open. Mr Miggins reached in and dragged Molly to the safety of the cage-room.

'Molly, are you all right?' he hugged his daughter to his chest.

Molly pulled away. 'I'm fine, Dad. I was just sealing the pit, but there was such a lot of wind in such a small space. I thought I was going to get sucked in.'

Granny Whitewand pushed past them and peered into what was left of the pit room.

The pit itself was gone, sealed off forever, covered with a pile of rock and dust that had fallen from the roof and walls.

'You made a bit of a mess in there, Millie,' Granny Whitewand cackled.

An enormous crashing sound came from above their heads.

'Everyone out!' shouted Mrs Miggins. 'The house is falling down.'

Mr Miggins picked up Henrietta and hauled her over his shoulder. 'Run, Molly,' he shouted.

Molly just made it out of the room as one of the walls came crashing down, splitting open barrels and spilling rotten apples over the floor. She took off her hat and ducked as she followed the hobbling, but amazingly quick figure of Granny Whitewand along the low passage. She had to wait at the bottom of the stairs while Granny Whitewand conjured up a levitation spell to help her get up them. Molly followed quickly, and leapt from the top step, into the kitchen as the staircase below her fell away.

Molly took Granny Whitewand's arm and helped her find a path across the brick-strewn kitchen floor, through the hall and out into what was, by now, almost a jungle of a garden. They stopped, puffing and panting, about ten yards away from the cottage. Molly heard an enormous cracking sound and looked back to see the roof split and sink in the middle. Another series of collapses followed as brick-dust and large splinters of fast-rotting wood flew into the air. Finally, the exterior walls collapsed inwards and what remained of the roof crashed down, leaving nothing but a pile of rubble.

'Well, that will save the bulldozer men some work,' said Granny Whitewand.

They stood in a group, surveying the wreckage of Cranberry Cottage for a few minutes, each of them lost in their own thoughts.

'I'm sorry it's gone,' said Molly, eventually. 'It was such a beautiful place.'

They collected their brooms and walked slowly down to the tall fence. The padlocks had fallen off at the moment Belladonna entered the pit. Great Aunt Willow pulled open one of the gates and they all stepped through onto the path beyond.

Henrietta began to stir as they got back to Great Aunt Willow's house.

'Molly Miggins, I know what you did. Thank you for coming to rescue me,' she mumbled, sleepily.

Molly leaned towards Mrs Miggins and whispered in her ear. 'Her dad will go mad when he finds out what happened to her.'

Mrs Miggins held her wand over Henrietta and cast a *Sleep* spell.

'That should sort it out, Molly. She'll wake up tomorrow thinking it was all a bad dream.' Molly pulled Wonky from her secret pocket and stood by the gate as the rest of the family walked up the garden path towards the house.

'Get the kettle on, Willow,' croaked Granny Whitewand. 'I'm parched.'

'Put it on yourself, Hazel,' said Aunt Willow. 'You haven't made tea once since you arrived.'

'You can tell that, because we haven't had a decent cuppa yet,' replied Granny Whitewand.

Their voices faded as they entered the house.

Molly addressed Wonky and sat down on the gate-step.

'Wonky, I don't tell you anywhere near often enough how wonderful you are, and how much I value your friendship and advice,' she said. 'I should tell you lots more than I do... it's not that I don't think it, and it's not that I take you for granted or anything.' She planted a kiss on the fat little face of the wand. 'You're the best wand in the whole, wide world, Wonky and I'm so lucky to have you as a partner.'

Wonky blushed.

'The feeling is mutual, Molly Miggins. I often think back to the day we met in the wand room. Fate threw us together. It was meant.' The wand smiled at Molly. 'Here's to many more adventures.'

'MOLLEEEEEEEEEEEEE!' Granny Whitewand's piercing screech forced its way out of the open kitchen door and sailed along the garden path.

'The Wizard is on the talky-conferencey thingy in the lounge. He wants a report and he's got a new task for you to start on Tuesday.'

Molly sighed and stood up.

'That's the thing, Wonky. We never have to wait very long for another adventure to come along, do we?'

Chapter Twenty-Two

Henrietta's father arrived, driven by his chauffeur, at ten o'clock the next morning. Henrietta had just finished a breakfast of boiled eggs, toast soldiers, and orange juice. She ran to her father's arms and gave him a hug at the front door.

Mr Havelots reached for his wallet. 'Thank you for letting her stay at such short notice. He offered a bundle of twenty-pound notes to Aunt Willow. 'This will cover any expenses incurred, I trust.'

'There's no need to pay me anything,' said Aunt Willow. 'Henrietta was very welcome.'

'I'll have it if you don't want it.' A long, bony hand reached out and snatched the notes from Mr Havelots hand. Granny Whitewand stuffed the money into her secret pocket.

'I'm almost out of bats wings, jellied newt's eyes and lizard's feet,' she explained. 'This will help me stock up.'

Mrs Miggins gave Molly a gentle push in the back and she reluctantly walked down to the car with the Havelots.

Henrietta stopped at the end of the garden and fidgeted, while staring hard at her fingers. 'I had such a strange dream last night. You were in it. You rescued me from an evil witch down at Cranberry Cottage.'

'Did I?' said Molly, trying not to get drawn into a conversation about the events of the night before. 'That must have been exciting.'

'It was scary,' replied Henrietta. 'I can't remember much about it now, only snippets, but I suppose I was very brave, I usually am, as you know. I just wish I could remember those bits, instead of...' she paused for a moment. 'I think I'll ask Dad to see if we can find Cranberry Cottage and take a photo of it. You do that sort of thing on your holidays, don't you? Take pictures to show people where you've been, and this place is quite famous, isn't it?'

'Oh I wouldn't bother taking a picture of Cranberry Cottage,' said Molly. 'It's just a pile of rubble now. The gardens are overgrown, there's nothing worth seeing.'

Henrietta scowled. 'I *KNEW* you were just making things up, Molly Miggins. I've wasted a whole weekend and all I've had out of it are a couple of boiled eggs and an hour or two in a stinky, fishy hovel. I'll tell the cook what I think of her family when I get back. I mean, they didn't even have a pony for me to ride.'

Henrietta got into the big car, slammed the door and pushed the button so that the electric window dropped down.

'I suppose I'll see you around and about, Molly Miggins.' She looked past Molly, out into the village street. 'There's something wrong somewhere, something I can't quite put my finger on, but I'm sure you're at the bottom of it. I'll remember one day, so you'd better hope it was something nice.' She paused for a moment, a frown on her brow. 'I keep getting the urge to say thank you, and that can't be right, can it? I mean, whatever could you possibly have done to earn my thanks? I hardly ever say thank you, and when I do it's only when I really, really have to, like when I've been given a nice, shiny present, but you haven't given me anything at all, have you?'

'No,' said Molly, 'not a thing. I can't imagine what could be making you feel like that.'

Henrietta sniffed. 'Ah well, it will pass, I suppose. Goodbye, Poor girl. See you, wouldn't want to be you.'

The car pulled off with a screech. Molly turned away and walked down to the village shop to buy sweets for the journey home.

*****

Mr Miggins, Molly and Great Aunt Willow pushed Granny Whitewand's huge, heavy trunk into the back of the people carrier car, then gave each other a farewell hug. Granny Whitewand herself waited at the rear door of the car. Mrs Miggins, who had already said her goodbyes to Aunt Willow, sat at the steering wheel as it was her turn to drive.

'Goodbye, Willow,' wailed Granny Whitewand. Tears streamed down her face.

Great Aunt Willow hugged her sister to her. Her cheeks were wet with her own tears.

'Promise me you'll come to visit soon,' sobbed Granny Whitewand. 'I'll miss you so much.'

'Not as much as I'll miss you,' sniffled Aunt Willow.

'I'll miss you more,' whispered Granny Whitewand.

'No you won't,' cried Aunt Willow.

Molly rolled her eyes and shook her head. She had seen this performance so many times over the years. She pressed the electric window switch and stuck her head out of the car before it had wound all the way down.

'Come on, Grandma. Aunt Willow is coming over to stay with us in two weeks' time.'

'It will seem like months,' wailed Aunt Willow and Granny Whitewand together.

Molly stuck her hand in her pocket, rustled the paper bag that held her caramel toffees, selected one, and stuck it into her mouth. Granny Whitewand was into her seat like a shot.

'Do you have a sweetie in your mouth, Millie?' she asked.

Molly shook her head. 'Nnnnoommff,' she replied.

The car pulled away leaving Aunt Willow waving by the side of the road. Molly waved, but Granny Whitewand's eyes never left her granddaughter's face.

'I don't believe you, Millie,' she said, and narrowed her eyes. 'Prove it, Say Rhinoceros.'

Molly swallowed her toffee and sighed. It was going to be a long drive home.

The End

Printed by Amazon Italia Logistica S.r.l.
Torrazza Piemonte (TO), Italy

13082969R00073